To R

Dream on!
Enjoy!

The Dreamers
Oliver Dahl

...I saw a knife spinning through the air, catching and reflecting the light of the dim bulbs. Everything seemed to slow down, like the air had turned to syrup. Once again I found myself wishing this were only a dream, and remembering that it was, but in my case, that fact didn't help me. The knife continued on its path toward me, the blade spinning up and down, end over end. I tried to turn and run, but I was frozen in place. I braced myself for the inevitable impact that would soon follow....

~**D**~

*Dedicated to my readers,
and may you enjoy this one.*

~**D**~

Copyright ©2011 by Oliver Dahl
All rights reserved. No part of this book may be reproduced in any form or by any means without permission in writing from the author, Oliver Dahl.

The Dreamers

A Story of Sam Kullen

Oliver Dahl

Oliver Dahl
Author's Note

Congratulations, you've picked up my novel, the Dreamers. This is a very interesting story for me. An important fact is, I wrote this book in the 2010 NaNoWriMo (National Novel Writers Month) pro-gram, though I came up with the idea long before. This program challenges writers over the nation to write a novel in only the month of November. I succesfully completed the challenge. If you count editing & publishing, then add a couple months, but....

This story is based on some of my experiences, my dreams. In Chapter 3, the dream Sam has about running through the jungle and hiding under tree roots, *I* actually had, although in my dream, there was a secret agent/terrorist guy, instead of a monster, and he "shot " me. When I woke up, I had a bruise in the same place he had "shot" me. This inspired the story that you are about to read.

This is not my first novel. I have written one other book so far, the Stone Chronicles: The

The Dreamers

Skeleton Curse. (The first book in the Stone Chronicles.) This book just had the opportunity to be published first. If you enjoy this book, I'm sure you'll enjoy my other book(s!) as well.

> Dream On!
> Oliver Dahl

Oliver Dahl

Introduction
An Excerpt from *The Dreamers' Handbook*

In the year 1910, March 31 to be exact, a relatively unknown author by the name of Edmund Huntle had a dream. Not an idea, nor a thought, but a night vision, a real dream.

This dream was so real, so vivid and clear, that he actually crossed over the boundary that separates our reality—earth—from where we go, or where our minds go, when we dream. A place he named the Dream Realm. In his dream, he learned how one could control or influence events on earth by shaping those events in the Dream Realm.

Edmund Huntle traveled the world, publishing his findings in newspapers, magazines, and psychology journals. His articles were ignored and mocked by all but a select few. Those few, under the guidance and direction of Edmund Hunt-

The Dreamers

le, formed a small group which became known as the Dreamers.

This group was made up of authors, artists, architects, engineers—brilliant creators with imaginations larger than what were previously thought possible. When they dreamed, whatever they dreamed became reality. With this new-found ability, they turned the impossible possible. They were changing the world for the better.

In April 1912, Edmund boarded a ship bound for America in search of more Dreamers. Four nights into the voyage, Edmund, quite by accident, dreamed the ship went down. That ship was the Titanic.

The details and events of that tragic voyage can be read about in history books, and even be seen in movies. Sadly, Edmund went down with the ship.

Due to the loss of Edmund, the Dreamers went underground. Several left the group completely, spooked by the possibilities that awaited in the Dream Realm.

Despite this tragedy, the Dreamers didn't give up. After much deliberation, they appointed another leader in 1914.

Once again, the Dreamers flourished in world rescue, daily, until the new leader dreamed about a world war.

Oliver Dahl

In the same year, his dream became true, just as Edmund Huntle before him. This "curse" plagued the leaders with a deadly grip.

Up until the twenty-first century, leader after leader of the Dreamers thrived, then failed.

Now, as times get more and more dire, the Dreamers are in need of more members.

That's where I come in.

The Dreamers

Oliver Dahl

Prologue

Steven Gallinger slipped between the aisles of bookshelves of the Stanford University library heading, towards archives. His master's thesis on brain activity during REM sleep for his psychology class wasn't due for a while, but he figured he could get a head start, anyway.

Upon reaching the archives, he started thumbing through some psychology journals circa 1910.

Steven began reading an article on dreams from some guy named Edmund Huntle.

Intriguing, he thought as he read. *But not possibly true.* He read the article anyway. This guy, Edmund, had somehow dreamed himself into a new world.

From that point on, Steven wished *he* could dream himself into a new world, leaving *this* one behind.

Something clicked—it felt right—destiny

The Dreamers

had chosen him.

Steven forgot about his master's thesis, brain activity, and REM sleep. He forgot about Stanford University, and everything he had to do in life.

He immersed himself into all of Edmund's writings, and all dream literature—fiction or not.

Trying to imagine the Dream Realm that Edmund had named and visited every night proved difficult, but from his writings, Steven soon had his own image of the Dream Realm in mind.

He imagined more things—what it would be like, who would be there—and all along, his imagination expanded.

And then, one night, the barrier between Steven and the Dream Realm dissolved.

It was greater than anything he had imagined before. The Dream Realm existed.

For the next three years, Steven explored it, observed it, and learned as much as he could about the Dream Realm. He earned himself a presence there, a life! In the Dream Realm he was free to do as he wished, how he wished. He became a leader, and then made himself emperor.

He was not alone.

The Dreamers found Steven, and offered him a place in their group. But he wouldn't give up his empire—he couldn't give up his new wondrous life. Everything he had always and ever wanted was his, now, in the Dream Realm. Popularity, glory—power! Even fame and fear of him! He wanted it, he could have it! Anything he desired could be his!

Steven's life dream was no longer to become a psychologist—dealing with everyone *else's* problems, he was an emperor of a foreign world!

Steven abandoned his old life, and slept instead. He was always in the Dream Realm, always emperor. And he loved it. He took on a new name. Malfix.

Though he rebuked the Dreamers' offer, he was intrigued by their abilities. They could control or influence things on earth!

Suddenly, the Dream Realm alone wasn't enough, he wanted the earth. Everything he had in the Dream Realm could be brought there! He could become emperor of *two* worlds!

He needed the Dreamers, he needed to find the source of their power, the power that allowed them to control things on earth, but he fought against them and their influence in the Dream Realm.

That was twelve years ago—this is now. Slowly, Malfix has been taking over the Dream Realm from the Dreamers, and cutting down the Dreamers' influence on others.

If he gains control of the entire Dream

The Dreamers
Realm, life as we know it will end. His idea of how things should be is not good—believe me.

I've seen it.

Oliver Dahl

Chapter 1

Hello, my name is Sam Kullen. My story begins at Chapman Middle School, in my arithmetic classroom, room two-oh-three. Just to let you know now, my mind was not on arithmetic—it never is. I'm a smart kid, but when I'm bored, well, I don't pay attention. Arithmetic is one of those boring classes and sometimes my imagination gets the best of me.

In school, I'm in the gifted-talented program. Even though my classes are accelerated, I still get bored sometimes.

I was sitting in the front row, staring at my teacher writing algorithms and equations on the whiteboard. I was pondering where my friend, Gabe was. I saw him before school, where he told me that he was ditching that day. Yes, you heard me right. Gabe was going to skip school. I wasn't too surprised by this; I simply doubted his courage to actually *do* it.

The Dreamers

Gabe and I are entirely different creatures. I'm good at school, and constantly get A's (in math class, mostly B's though). While Gabe, well, he likes to talk about skipping school and putting stink bombs in the teachers' desks.

He hadn't shown up to third period; the only period he and I shared, I knew he must have been serious about ditching. It was now seventh period, and I hadn't seen him in the halls or at lunch. He hadn't lied. He had not come to school.

I glanced at the clock; the school day was over in forty seconds. I put my pencils in my binder and was zipping it closed when Mrs. Trell said: "Sam, the bell hasn't rung yet. You will stay five minutes after."

I hated her high pitched, whiny voice, and her tight, tawny face. Heck, I didn't even like her name! It sounded like troll! I could imagine her morphing into a green, ugly, Star-Wars-worthy creature, wrecking havoc and destroying cars and buildings. She'd be meters tall, and not even the FBI could defeat her! And—well, that goes to show how my imagination can get carried away. Oh well.

Trying not to roll my eyes as Mrs. Trell erased the white board, (which was covered in complicated algorithms) I stopped putting my stuff away in my binder.

Oliver Dahl

The bell rang and the class was dismissed. Everybody, but me. I earned several sneers and snickers from my classmates.

Mrs. Trell looked at me, obviously annoyed that by having me stay, she too, had to stay.

"You can go," Mrs. Trell sighed.

I headed to my locker to grab my science report and backpack, then walked through the double release doors.

My bus wouldn't leave for another ten minutes, so I looked around for Gabe. He told me he'd meet me after school was out, next to the back park bench (our meeting place).

And, what do you know, there he was, grinning like an idiot. (Gabe might be in the seventh grade, but he rarely showered. It was obvious. He usually had dirt on his face, and his hair was a black mess.)

Despite his lack of cleanliness, he was a pretty fun guy. Is he a bit immature for his age? Sure. Juvenile delinquent? Maybe. But he's a loyal friend and he puts up with me.

His parents are both police officers, which may explain some of his behavioral issues.

Gabe's parents are at work most of the time, so he does practically whatever he wants. I envy him in some ways. But my life is pretty good, too.

I have a younger sister, and that's it. Me and

The Dreamers

my little sis, Cynthia. She's four years old and can make a heck of a lot of noise for a preschooler. Then again, she's the only preschooler I know, so how do I know if she's quiet compared to the other little kids?

Maybe the other kids have siren-like *whisper* voices, and when they get mad it blows their room to smithereens! And when they talk, their glass spills all over the table and puts Cynthia to shame! Cynthia would be considered "quiet," then. And what if...?

There I go again. Sorry. Back to Gabe.

As I walked to the bench, I couldn't help but laugh and shake my head.

"How is it that both of your parents are cops, and you're still a jerk?" I rolled my eyes when he impersonated my voice. He did it just to annoy me. He did a pretty good job.

As usual Gabe smiled and shrugged.

"So… what did you do today, other than play hooky?" I asked, curious.

"Oh, I went to a movie—that new one that you want to see. Then I snuck into my dad's car and ate his jelly doughnuts,"

At this, I knew he was joking. Both of his parents were on a strict diet, and they stayed away from sugar of any kind.

Gabe was supposed to be on the diet too,

but, being Gabe, he always managed to get candy and stuff.

"No, really." I asked, rolling my eyes.

"Well, actually, I didn't do much, today." He said. "I've been feeling kind of sick. It's almost a good thing, because I had forgotten that on Thursdays my mom and dad come back to the house for lunch.

"They saw me and thought I was playin' hooky. But when they saw my green face and my sweaty jacket, they knew that I was sick. They said they'd call the doctor, but I told 'em I'd be okay. They went back to work and left me. As soon as they left, I felt better. So I went out, and did see that movie. That I wasn't jokin' about."

I nodded and shrugged. I was jealous that he saw "Space Exploration without me." I had been itching to see that for weeks.

"Space Exploration" is sort of a franchise of movies, books, action figures, video games, and other merchandise. It's pretty popular among middle school boys. But I heard it *is* the best movie ever created.

Both Gabe and I have "Space Exploration" 1-3 on PlayStation. It's pretty cool. I spent a month during summer vacation on it. Beat it. Gabe had to have one more week with my help, but he beat it too.

The Dreamers

"Space Exploration 3" is probably the only video game I've ever beat Gabe at completing.

As the buses began to turn on their engines, Gabe and I jogged back to them, immediately remem-bering that we had to be home on time.

Gabe and I were on different buses, because we went to neighboring subdivisions. We had met at school, in sixth grade, and were friends after a particularly rowdy food fight in the cafeteria when an eighth grade girl got pegged in the face with a particularly green and bouncy....

Never mind—don't get me started.

The bus slowed down then stopped for me.

My house was at the other end of the block. I walked down the street, up the sidewalk to the door, and I was home.

I arrived at my house—an ordinary two-story house with a small yard full of dandelions—to quite a surprise! I nearly rubbed my eyes in astonishment. Could what I be seeing *really* be in front of me? It didn't seem possible! There was no fuel for it, plus, it defied physics!

Above the alcove over the front door was a fancy-lettered "D" suspended in the air. And if that wasn't weird enough, the "D" was on fire! I looked around to see if any of the other kids from the bus had seen it, but the street was empty.

This was only the beginning.

Chapter 2

I ran inside my house, calling to my mom to come out—quick.

"Mom! Oh my gosh! Come outside quick!"

Startled that something was wrong, she followed me out. I pointed at the flaming "D" above our house.

"T-tell me you see that!" I stammered.

"See what, honey?" She asked, confused.

"Look where I'm pointing!"

"Honey, I don't see anything!" As you can see, she's big on "honey". It gets annoying at times, but I don't really care. It's not as if I can really do anything about it, either. It's just one of her annoying habits.

"Sam, what are you playing at?" she asked, tiredly, this time. "I don't have time for this." She rubbed her forehead the way she always does when she gets tired. The sides of her face seem to get heavier, her eyebrows droop, and the corners of her

The Dreamers

mouth follow suit. This is her "stressed" face. Unfortunately, she has to wear it a lot.

She sighs and walks back inside. I hesitate and look at the "D" in bewilderment.

After my mother had returned to the house, the "D" burned itself out of existence. *What in the...?*

Bewildered, I, too, followed my mother back inside. I tried to wash the image from my mind by hitting my head on my pillow, but, of course, that works like trying to catch a fly in your mouth, (don't ask).

I wandered down the stairs and got a drink of orange juice from the fridge. My mother was preparing dinner. She asked, "Are you feeling okay?" I sighed and replied miserably, "I don't know."

"You want to lay down for a bit?"

"No—mom, I'm okay, I don't need a nap, I'm not sick, I'm just..." I searched for an explanation. "Stressed" I finish lamely. I hoped the excuse would fly. I knew I hadn't imagined the "D". It was much too vivid to have been a hallucination. Of course, I'd never had a hallucination before, so, who was I to say that they weren't vivid?

"Okay, then. If you need anything, just ask, okay honey?"

Oliver Dahl

"Alright, Mom." I say tiredly. Once again, I walk up the stairs to my room and lay on my bed. I send a text message to Gabe. I could think of nothing better to do, and I was bored.

"What's up?"

He replied instantly.

"Dud, we jus talkd" Gabe misspells words and uses text language, and I can't stand it. I always spell my words out, and I hardly ever use text talk.

"I know… I'm bored." I text back, lamely.

"OK…"

"Never mind." I finish. I jump off my bed and swing into my desk chair. I survey my room—taking in all the posters and drawings that I've collected over the years. There's hardly a part of my wall that's not covered. I rip off an old doodle and trash it. I decide to replace it with something better. My result is a fairly good sketch of my house, with a bright, burning, glowing "D" on top of it.

Several times as I sketch, I close my eyes to remember more clearly. My house is hard enough to draw, but I know it well. It's the flames that give me trouble. As I work, I find myself with an okay house, but the "D" looks a little fake. I shrug, and continue working.

When I'm done, I feel satisfied with it. It's

The Dreamers

actually pretty good. Ever since I was a little kid, I liked drawing, writing, and building stuff, things like that. I call myself a "builder" for that reason. I can't stand destroying things. That's why I only rarely buy building toys. I can't take them apart once I assemble them.

Soon thereafter, my mom calls me down to dinner. Cynthia is already seated happily, smiling away. My mother gives me a burrito.

"It should be good for your cold, Sam, eating, I mean."

"Mom," I sigh, "I don't have a cold. I'm fine, really." She shakes her head, obviously not believing me. We finish dinner in relative silence.

Yup. I'm fine, except I had experienced some sort of hallucination.

Though I constantly looked above my bedside window to see if another "D" had appeared, I didn't see it again. I was half relieved, and half worried.

Finally, sick at myself for this stupid behavior, I sat down on my bed, pulled up the sheets, and lied down. I pondered what I had seen, ques-tioning my sanity. It *must* have been a hallucination. I rolled over, exhausted.

I soon fell asleep, and experienced my first dream.

Chapter 3

It was dark. It was green. It was moist. I couldn't see very far, but what I did see amazed me. Tall twisty, vine-like trees grown at violent angles. Several thick vines woven together created the trunks.

There was a steam in the air, like after a long, hot shower. It swirled like a living thing, floating this way and that.

The thick foliage banned much of the light from coming through, making it almost appear to be night time.

All around me, chatters and howls, roars and hisses surrounded me like walls in a room.

My heart started pounding, I didn't like where I was, *wherever* I was... I shivered despite the heat.

The hairs on my neck tingled, and my stomach contracted. I couldn't take it. I ran, ran for all I was worth.

The Dreamers

I could hear heavy breathing behind me. Thick, like a bear was breathing through a mattress. Whatever was chasing me was big... and probably fast.

My lungs ached and my legs screamed. I ran harder, I ran faster. The sweat from my brow trailing behind me.

Finally, I stopped, ducking behind a tree. Some of its large roots were exposed, forming a small crevice. Desperate, I slid inside, breathing hard, fast, and very unevenly.

I could hear the monster. Its footsteps shook the earth—if that's what planet I was on!

I had a nasty feeling it could hear me, too. I tried, I tried so hard to control my breathing, but I couldn't. I couldn't get enough oxygen.

Thump, thump, thump, the monster *had* heard me and was coming closer. His breathing nearly drowned mine out, that's how loud it was!

It let out a deep, guttural roar that reverberated around the jungle and almost made my eardrums hurt.

I shut my eyes tight, bracing myself against the tree roots, waiting for it to be torn from its roots and for me to be killed by a giant alien-bear thing.

But it never came. Instead, I heard a profound clash, and another roar. I peered over the edge of my impromptu hideout, hoping not to lose my head.

Somebody, or something, was trying to stop the bear. And if they were trying to stop the bear, they were probably on my side.

I jumped up, tripping over my heels to get out of the confined space.

"Hey! Hey! I'm over here!" I shouted desperately. "Help!"

A projectile whizzed past my head and I dropped again. Maybe these guys weren't on my team.

I felt something graze my left arm, level with my heart. I realized that whoever was out there was shooting arrows at me! Arrows!

Great, I thought. From one trouble to another. Almost rolling my eyes, I took off again, running away from the direction that the arrows had come... waiting for the one that wouldn't miss.

I streaked through the jungle, my stiff muscles complaining. *If I make it through this, I'm going to be sore for a month,* I thought.

And then I broke through.

I was teetering on the edge of an outcropping of boulders at the top of a large cliff. I looked down. Big mistake. I almost lost my balance. Whatever was at the bottom I'm sure wouldn't be a soft landing.

The Dreamers

Trying to avoid this fate, I ran back into the jungle.

"Could this get any worse?" I asked, as I saw my pursuers caught in a web, and three large spiders looking up at me. Their fangs foamed and their hairs bristled with excitement.

"This is like a horror show with no intermission..." I muttered, shaking my head.

I made my decision. I decided that, in death, I'd rather jump to it, than let giant, black spiders lead me to it.

As I ran back to the cliff ledge, I ignored my sore muscles, my bruised and cut legs, and the arrow graze on my shoulder.

I looked off the cliff again, beginning to doubt my theory. Nevertheless, I jumped.

My heart, being so high in my throat in the first place, should have come shooting out my head, but it didn't. As if it would matter.

The breeze blew up my pajama pant legs and through my shirt, chilling me to the bone.

And then I stopped. I was surrounded by blue light, like a lightning bolt. It seemed to be suspending me.

I slowly found myself being raised along the side of the cliff.

What's next, aliens? I thought with dread.

Instead, I found myself face to face with

another human being. He wore a white jump suit, with a fancy-lettered "D" on it.

I gasped. "The 'D'! What does it mean? Why am I here? What is this place?"

I felt like the Hoover Dam had just broke, and instead of water came questions.

To my surprise, the man answered me, and didn't light me on fire or anything.

"The 'D' is the symbol for the Dreamers, a secret society of authors, artists, engineers, and people with vivid imaginations.

"You are here because you are a Dreamer. You are one of us.

"This place is called the Dream Realm, and that jungle you just ran out of is a territory of the most evil man in existence, Malfix. Satisfied?"

I could do nothing but nod. "Well, What's that got to do with me...?" I was at a loss for words, confused by this strange man.

The man smiled stiffly.

"I'm Thep. I live in Egypt, on earth. And you are?"

"Sam," I said, making it sound more like a question. He smiled that same way again.

He sighed, then spoke quickly in his deep, barely accented voice "Well Sam, you've got a lot to learn. It will take some time, but you must listen, press forward, and do everything I say.

The Dreamers

Don't every question anything that comes out my mouth. Understand?"

I nodded, overwhelmed with new information from this virtual stranger.

"Good. We shall start off with Malfix. Malfix is—"

"The most evil man in existence." I interrupted, again saying it sort of like a question. I didn't know anything, anymore, it seemed.

Thep nodded, annoyed with my interruption.

"Yes, and he is trying to take over the Dream Realm. Once he does that, he will be able to control people on earth through their dreams. With that ability, he will connect the Dream Realm to earth, allowing him to rule the universe.

"Our job is to stop him. It is simple enough, I think."

I nodded again, a confused expression on my face.

"How did I get here? How do I return?" I asked.

"You dream, and did dream. Meet me at ten o' clock, sharp. Don't tell anyone." He replied, with the same smile on his face.

At that point, everything blurred white, and Thep's dark face mixed into it all like mixing paint.

My alarm clock blared. I winced at the noise. My eyes didn't want to open, my mouth was dry, and I needed a tissue. I rubbed my face, and stretched my shoulders. I breathed deeply in and out, and rolled my ankles. And then I remembered.

What a crazy dream!

The Dreamers
Chapter 4

School wasn't the same. If I couldn't concentrate before, I sure couldn't concentrate now. Thep's words echoed in my mind.

Malfix is the most evil man in existence... You are here because you are a Dreamer; you are one of us... Meet me at ten o' clock, sharp. Don't tell anyone.

His words haunted me, but first and foremost, were the injuries. All day I was terribly sore, and my pajama shirt was bloody when I had woken up. A thin scabbed scar that I had never had before lay directly underneath my shirt where the arrow had grazed my left arm. As if that weren't strange enough, it was just a scar! When I'd talked with the old guy, Thep, it was bleeding! I examined the rest of myself. I found several more injuries, though not quite as pressing as my arm.

My feet were scratched up, and bruised, from the tree roots, no doubt.

Oliver Dahl

Of course, these physical reminders didn't help answer any of my questions, like, "How do we stop Malfix," or just, "What the h-e-double hockey-sticks is going on!"

All day, even in art class, I couldn't pay attention. By the end of the day, I wanted to run home as fast as I could, and sleep and return to dream land, or wherever.

I simply couldn't stand not knowing what was going on. Everything in my life had changed. No longer would my biggest worries in life be late math homework and basketball tryouts. I tried to sort out the details.

So, first off, I was apparently part of some secret organization trying to save the world.

Secondly, the Dream Realm had some evil guy, Maxfly? No... Malfix, who was bent on controlling people on earth via their dreams. How was that even possible?! And we're supposed to stop him? *How?*

In Mrs. Trell's seventh period, without even thinking, I began packing early again. Of course, she had to look my way.

This earned me another five minutes after the bell with her. I couldn't believe it! If I could tell her I was a member of a group trying to save her butt from being controlled by an evil warlord, then she might have given me a second consideration.

The Dreamers

Who am I kidding? If I tell her that, she'll set up an appointment with a school counselor and tell him I'm crazy.

Maybe in the end, I'll make *her* spend five minutes in Malfix's control.

Finally, after that was over, and I promised "never to do it again," I could leave. I had some questions I needed to ask Thep. My mom was parked in the parking lot and waved me over quickly.

My mom picks me up every other day from school, because she had to work on the days in between. It was silly, I didn't mind riding the bus.

But, every other school day, I climb in the back of our Suburban for the short drive home.

I ruffled Cynthia's hair as she sat in her booster. She started telling me all about her day and the projects she had done in school. I couldn't get a word in edgewise.

The whole half-minute drive, I stared impatiently at the clock and the speedometer, willing the speedometer needle to dramatically rise, and the clock to speed ahead about four hours If only it were that simple.

We finally pulled up to our driveway, (imagine that!) and parked in the garage. Our garage is full of camping gear. My dad loves to camp. He says it's to "get away from it all," but with all of his gear, I don't know what exactly he's getting away from.

I walked inside our house, ignoring the mailbox that I usually check. I looked at the microwave clock. Just before four. That was six hours until I was supposed to meet Thep in Dreamland, or wherever. My shoulders hunched.

"Honey, are you okay?" I sighed and my shoulders hunched further down.

"Mom...I'm fine. It's just..." *just that I'm supposed to save the world from a horrible and horrific fate.* I thought.

"What's for dinner?" I asked, changing the subject.

"Chicken noodle soup, I think it'll be good for your...cold."

I groaned. "Mom! I'm fine! Really."

I stomped up to my room and sat on my unmade bed, pulling off my backpack and dropping it to the floor.

I pulled out my homework and began working on that. My mind wasn't on diagramming sentences, or doing eight-step fraction problems. I didn't see how homework was ever going to help me in life. It wasn't as if I'd really use eight-step equations flipping burgers at a burger joint, or using diagrammed sentences when I become an artist or engineer.

The Dreamers

The only job I could come up with that would require knowledge of complicated equations, was a math teacher, or if you were Steve Jobs or Bill Gates. (Or, for diagrammed sentences, an English teacher, but....)

Anyway, time passed on, and pressure in my head increased. I ate the chicken noodle soup, more out of politeness than actual need, though. Don't get me wrong, chicken noodle soup is good, but not as much when you're waiting for a secret group meeting concerning the fate of the world.

Two hours later, I sat in bed, staring at my digital bedside alarm clock, counting the seconds to 8:42. It was going to be a long night. I sighed with dread at what was to come.

At one point, just after nine, my mom came in and touched my forehead. "Are you sure you're okay? You are usually still up playing, who-knows-what on your laptop."

I sighed again, and, as if it would make her happier, replied. "You know Mom, I think I do have a cold." I then added, "I think the chicken soup is helping." She smiled.

"Good." She kissed my forehead, (I know, I know) and left my room, shutting the door quietly behind her.

Good night, I thought.

Oliver Dahl
Chapter 5

The setting was totally different this time. This place appeared to be like an Arctic wasteland. It was covered in snow and ice. To my dismay, I noticed that I was again wearing only my pajamas. They consisted of a Blue Angel's T-shirt that used to be my Dad's, and sweats. Normally warm and comfy, but not when it came to Antarctica.

I groaned. I had fallen asleep around nine thirty, nearly thirty minutes too early. I didn't want to wait thirty minutes *here*. It was, well...cold. I shivered, and heard laughing behind me.

"Thought you'd be early." Thep had that same stiff smile on his face.

Of course, I had to make a fool of myself and ask a stupid question first.

"Wait, if you live in Egypt, then isn't your time zone different than mine?"

Thep smiled a real smile this time.

"That is a simple question with a complicat-

The Dreamers

ed answer." The way he said it made it sound like that was his answer. His tone precluded any follow-up questions.

Of course.

"Well, no time to waste time." Thep said, chiming in as if it were his motto. "Let's begin. We shall first discuss who we are, what we do, and what our goals are. Sound fair?"

I nodded, eager to learn more, ready to assure myself that last night's dream wasn't just a dream.

"We are Dreamers. Our goal is to stop Malfix from taking over the world. The Dreamers are a secret group of authors, architects, engineers, artists, and people with very...overactive and vivid imaginations.

"Our imaginations are so strong that they break through the barrier between reality and dream. We break through each time we dream, as soon as we come of age. This does not literally mean that when you turn thirteen, you are a Dreamer, or not. Coming of age simply means that your imagination has finally grown strong enough to break through the barrier. This can happen at random times. Theoretically, you could come of age while you are four years old, but that has only happened once..."

Wanting answers, I sure seemed to have

found them, but all of this information was beginning to spin through my head like a carousel on overdrive.

"This is the Dream Realm, discovered in our age by a man named Edmund Huntle. I say 'our age' because Edmund didn't create it; he found it, in the early 1900's. Up until the early '90's, the Dream Realm was a pretty peaceful place. A young psychology student from Stanford forced his way into the Realm and has been causing trouble ever since. Malfix. He used to just come here as an escape from his mundane life... we all have our own dreams.

"Malfix changed from wanting asylum to wanting power. Our society tried early on to recruit him, to make it easier to keep tabs on him. It only drove him away.

"Once he saw what us Dreamers could do, he wanted that power all to himself. He's been trying to destroy us ever since.

"We've been involved in a war with him for a while now. We win some battles, we lose others. Currently, he has control of four out of the seven territories that make up the Dream Realm. If he takes the other three, he'll be able to merge the Dream Realm with earth. Once he does that, if he does, he'll be able to control people on earth through their dreams."

The Dreamers

"But how—?" I interrupted.

"It's complicated," Thep replied, holding his hand up to prevent further questions.

"As we speak, Malfix controls Paradisa, the Ceruvian Sea, the Death Regions, and that jungle you visited last night, the Jungle of Arac Mad. We have a somewhat tenuous, jeopardized control over the areas known as Futurecon, the Ice Caves, and the Floating Peaks.

"Futurecon, Death Regions, Paradisa?" I asked. "Floating Peaks?"

"Yes, Futurecon is a futuristic city with quite a population. We think he'll attack there, next. He needs to build an army. The Death Regions is a vast wasteland on the surface, but is riddled with natural resources and many raw materials Malfix is using to equip his army.

"Paradisa is exactly its cognate. Paradise. It's different for everyone. When you dream about the perfect place, you go to Paradisa. For some, it's a mountain lake, for others, it's a beach with palm trees and beautiful sunsets. Just watch out for the sand crabs. Nasty little buggers." Thep looked off into the distance as though remembering something from long ago.

"Okay... what about the other ones? The Ice Caves, Ceruvian Sea and the peaks?" I prompted.

"Well," Thep continued, brought back to the

Oliver Dahl

present by my question. "We're close to the Ice Caves, the Ceruvian Sea is beyond them, and is huge. The Floating Peaks are... peaks that float."

"Well, yeah, I'd figured that..." I trailed off, blushing. The cold was seeping into my marrow.

"They're like hills floating in the air. It looks like a giant was trying to transplant flowers, and just put the dirt in the air. It's beautiful, really. Shame they don't have them on Earth."

Everything was silent but the loud, hissing wind.

"The Floating Peaks actually house our main head quarters. And that's where we need to go. You're lucky you didn't dream yourself back into the jungle like you did last night. Our spies tell us he's been tearing the place apart, hoping to find you.

"What? Why?" I asked, perplexed.

"I was hoping to have this conversation somewhere warmer, but I guess there's no time like the present." Thep continued by asking, "Have you ever had the same dream?"

"Huh?" I was perplexed. What did that have to do with anything?

"Have you ever dreamed that you're in the same place you have been before?"

"Well, yeah. I dream all the time that I'm camping with my dad and we forget to bring the tent. And that I'm in this weird house thing, and it's always the same plot."

"Good. We often have re-run dreams or repeats. Something in our mind triggers a replay of the same, or nearly the same, dream." Thep explained.

"That's why Malfix is looking high and low for you in that jungle of his. He's hoping that you'll show up again."

"But why?" I asked, getting frustrated.

"There hasn't been a new Dreamer for years, particularly one as young as you. The Dreamers that remain are definitely not as young as we used to be. Our time is limited in the Dream Realm—and on earth. The less time we have to spend here in the Dream Realm fighting Malfix, the more powerful he becomes. Teenagers, such as yourself can sleep for ten to twelve hours, maybe even more. Plus, you have your whole life ahead of you! You have a lot of potential time in the Dream Realm. Us senior citizens don't get as much sleep as we'd like."

Thep's face was identical to the one he had used when describing sand crabs in Paradisa—a longing, remembering, thoughtful face.

"Anyway, the more we wake up, the less time we spend here, fighting Malfix.

"So, if Malfix could simply get you on his

side, it would almost be the end of us. We're near ending enough as it is."

Thep paused, then continued.

"Now, before we die of hypothermia or get frostbite, grab my arm."

"But wh—"

Things were weird enough, already. Standing in the middle of a freezing desert in Dreamland, it almost made sense that by grabbing a guy's arm, you could appear somewhere else.

I grabbed his arm, and off we went.

The Dreamers
Chapter 6

It was like riding a roller coaster through a rainbow, but not that cheesy. Oops, scratch that, it was like riding a roller coaster on a spinning *teacup ride* through a rainbow.

It was crazy and disorienting, but before I knew it, I was standing on a large green and grassy mountain range. I had a hunch as to where I was.

I looked down and saw that we were standing on one of the Floating Peaks. There were dozens and dozens of them, ranging in size from a school bus to a mountain. They were just... floating!

"Before we go inside, there's something you should know." Thep said after I had taken the time to process the fact that we were floating a few hundred feet off the ground.

"Our leader, who you'll meet in a few moments, is dying. He doesn't like to admit it, but he's likely to live only a few more weeks. He has spent the last decade fighting Malfix, and it has taken its toll. That, and he wasn't exactly young to begin with."

"So, if a person dies in the Dream Realm, do they die on earth, too?" I asked.

"It's complicated." Thep replied. A standard fallback for Thep, I had learned.

"Have you ever fallen, or been hurt in a dream?" Thep asked.

I responded with the affirmative, "Of course, all the time."

"Ah, but when you awoke, you were fine, right?"

"Right...."

"Well, now, as a Dreamer, that's going to change. Any injury we sustain in the Dream Realm —as a Dreamer—will affect our bodies on earth.

"You've already experienced this. The wound you received last night in the jungle..."

"Yeah, I woke up with dried blood on my pajamas and a scar," I said, rubbing my arm through the shirtsleeve.

"Wounds received hear heal quickly there, but they are still wounds, and over time, can add up."

Thep continued. "When normal people dream that they get hurt, fall, or die, usually they just wake up startled. No problem. But, when we as 'Dreamers,'" he made the little quote marks with

The Dreamers

his fingers in the air, (overkill, if you ask me) "get hurt, fall, or die, something else happens."

"Like my scar?"

"Like your scar." Thep affirmed. "Now, if I were to push you off this peak, and you splatted on the ground below, as a Dreamer, you would die here," he paused for effect, "*and* there."

"But... how?"

"Think about it. Is your body here, or at home, in bed?"

"Uh... in bed?"

"Right, but now you're a Dreamer, and instead of just having part of your mind or subconsciousness here, *you* are here. I guess you could call it your essence. I don't know that it has a name. Honestly, *you're* the only one who's ever asked this many questions about it all. But your essence is more than just your mind—which is why when you got nicked with that arrow last night, you bled. And that's why if you, as a Dreamer, die in the Dream Realm, you yourself will die."

It seemed as if it was noon here, and the sun shone brightly in the sky.

Thep was right, it was beautiful. I could imagine butterflies flitting about, and deer grazing in a nearby meadow. This could be on a postcard. I'd have to remember to wear a camera to bed tomorrow, although, nobody would believe that I'd taken the pictures.... Sorry... imagination again.

I smiled and rolled my eyes. I then turned and was confronted with a lady in her forties or fifties with dark black hair and a white... lab coat?

"Sam, how wonderful it is to meet you. I trust Thep has treated you well, and taught you the basics?" She directed these questions to Thep, but I answered for her.

"Yeah." She pursed her lips at this, and I immediately didn't like her too much.

"Very well then, follow me. I'll take you for a little...tour." She said simply. "I'm Victoria, by the way, Sam."

"Oh," was all I could say. She pursed her lips again, and opened what looked like a door to an outhouse. I was sure she knew Thep, because how else would she know my name?

Inside was a concrete staircase that led to the heart of this floating peak. I followed Victoria down. The staircase went down about ten steps, and then turned left at a 180-degree angle, and continued further down another ten steps, until you ended directly under where you started. I counted about eight flights until we stopped. My legs were still sore from my jungle trip, and this didn't help.

So far, I wasn't impressed with the Dreamers' headquarters. It seemed like a prison. I contin-

The Dreamers

ued to follow Victoria down a long, cement hallway with dim light bulbs illuminating it. I frowned. It was cold, too. I did not want to spend much more time here.

"And here, Sam, is where the magic happens." Victoria said with a tight smile. She opened a heavy metal door and an amazing sight lay before me.

It was like mission control in the movies, but on a grander scale. Computers hummed, and the sound of people typing echoed in the near-silent room with the sound of beeps and boops.

The strange thing was, everything from medieval swords and spears, to modern day machine guns and RPG's lined the walls on all sides. Small slits in the walls allowed for shooting outside of the room.

A man pushed by us, I may have seen his picture in the jacket of a book I had read. He ran up to an old man in a fancy chair.

"Sir! There's—"

"Don't call me sir," The man said kindly. "Isaac will do just fine." Somehow, I had seen him before, *somewhere*.

"It's an emergency, one of Malfix's exploring parties must have seen us let the boy and Thep in, their opening fire on us now. We have to wake them up from their dreams or they will know where our headquarters are! What should we do to stop them?"

The man looked sad and weary. He sighed sadly. "I hate when we have to revert to this." He muttered.

"Prepare to open fire on the exploring party below us. In this setting, they may be our enemies, however, they are just every-day people whose dreams have been hijacked by Malfix He's controlling them to get to us."

I felt that this explanation was more for my benefit than the others, as I had no idea what was going on.

"Because they aren't Dreamers, when they die in the Dream Realm, they will simply wake up in their beds from a nightmare." The man, obviously the leader of the Dreamers, said sadly.

It was obviously a practiced drill. The Dreamers all jumped up from their seats and ran to weapons on the wall. Some grabbed bows, or crossbows, others grabbed machine guns, or pistols.

I remained frozen as the once-quiet room exploded into action.

I found myself pushed to a window and I discovered that I probably had the best view in the place.

The sound of gunfire and of bows being

The Dreamers

plucked and arrows hissing through air replaced the relatively quiet sound of the office, with typing and stuff.

Within seconds, the entire exploring party vanished like a fading spark. Tendrils of smoke curled up and twisted through the faint breeze from the nearby windows. The Dreamers simply replaced their weapons and went back to what they were working on before.

The exploring party had vanished into thin air.

And suddenly, as if the smoke was sleepi— waking up gas, there was that swirling white mixed with all the other colors, and I awoke.

Oliver Dahl

Chapter 7

Sitting up straight, I noticed the space around me smelled slightly like smoke. My hair was messy, I could tell. Once again, my mouth was dry. I ran downstairs to get some water. It was Saturday, thank goodness. I didn't have school and could go back to bed. I sighed. Sleeping to save the world. Weird.

I got a large glass of water, and went back upstairs. I took a deep breath and lied back down. Under my sheets, I stared at the ceiling and watched my room get lighter and lighter.

Sleep evaded me. My mind and body were tense. I was anything *but* relaxed. I tossed and turned, thinking about what had just happened. So much that my head hurt. Then, I finally found that comfy position that I could relax and fall back asleep in. Shortly after, I dozed off.

~D~

The Dreamers

I was relieved when I showed up in head quarters, and not in some jungle or in Antarctica. I spotted Thep and moved toward him. He was speaking with the leader—Isaac, but when he saw me approaching, he looked surprised.

"We didn't expect to see you again so soon after you woke up. I'm glad you're back. We've got a lot of work to do. Malfix is up to something, and that's not good. We've been able to determine he's in Futurecon, so you, Flitch, and I are going to go check it out."

Before I realized I was speaking, I asked a bunch of questions.

"How do you know where Malfix is? What's he up to? What can we do about it? And who is Flitch?"

Thep held up his hand to stem the flow of my curiosity.

"One thing at a time—unfortunately, we don't have a lot of that, though. I'll explain as much as I can as we go.

"First off, all the people you see here are tasked with keeping tabs on Malfix and those he uses. Sometimes we go weeks without so much as a clue, then we'll get lucky and get a lock on him. Part of our organization is dedicated to gather information or intelligence—kind of like the CIA. With all of the amazingly creative minds at our disposal, we've been able to develop computer programs, tracking software, and a spy network the CIA itself could only dream of. In fact, that's exactly how we got it.

"Anyway, our spies indicate Malfix is about to do something. Exactly what? We're not sure—that's why we're going to check it out. Flitch is a member of the team. He's a bit eccentric but handy to have around—good for... comic relief. And backup, of course." Thep added as an afterthought. I got the idea that this afterthought was *supposed* to be this Flitch guy's job.

Thep looked to the older man sitting on the fancy chair (could it be a throne?). The old man, Isaac, nodded.

Thep handed me a... a....

"What's this?" I asked.

"It's a stun gun. We use it if we run into trouble."

"Trouble? What kind of trou—"

"You'll know it if you see it. In fact, they'll probably see you first. If we can't avoid them, our orders are to stun them and bring them back here for questioning. If we stun them, their bodies on earth can't wake up," Thep added, seeing the question forming on my lips.

He continued. "If we can avoid them, that's great. But the plan is to get in, see what's going on, and get out without being seen, if that's at all possible."

"If you see a man in black and green, tell me. We'll stun them, bring 'em back here, and interrogate them. That's all we need to do. But then, if Malfix *is* investigating things, then our job continues. We'll have to hope he's not. Sound like a plan?"

It was confusing, and I was kind of like, TMI, dude. But I nodded.

"But... if they are 'just dreaming' what good will it do to question them? Aren't they just normal people on earth?"

"Yes, they are normal people, but Malfix has captured their minds, and controlled their dreams to help him build an army. What good will it do? Malfix informs, and tells the people he controls what they need to do, and occasionally, why. If we can get this information from them, we're set."

"Wait... but if people on earth know about Malfix's plans, then wouldn't they be able to know about the Dream Realm, or would they think that it was 'just a dream' or...?"

"So many 'buts' and questions...." Thep muttered.

"Although, I think you know the answer to this question. As a non-Dreamer, they dream every single night, just like us. They just don't think so, as they *can't remember* sometimes, what they have dreamed. They forget."

"O-o-o-oh...." I mused.

"Do *we* forget what we dream?" I asked.

"No, no. Since our essences are actually *in* the Dream Realm, we remember everything as if we had been here personally. In a way, we almost *are* here personally."

I may have asked more questions, but Thep stopped me.

"Well then, I'll let you meet Flitch now, but let me warn you...he's an...interesting character."

Thep led me out of mission control into a smaller room on the left-hand side of the hall. He opened the door, and with a dramatic flourish of his hands, waved me in.

It was a simple room. A small, portable desk, a laptop, and, surprisingly, a bed consisted of the room's scant furniture. And, of course there was that Flitch guy. Weird name for a weird dude.

First off, he had long hair, and wrinkles on his face that showed he smiled a lot. He had vibrant eyes that seemed to be a gateway to another world.

As he saw me examine him, he laughed a big, hearty laugh that seemed practiced, and smooth. "Boy, are you sizing me up? 'Cause if you are planning on fighting me, you'll probably win."

The Dreamers

It took me a while to comprehend. It wasn't that funny, just a twist of a stereotypical phrase.

Flitch sounded to me like Jay Leno. He didn't really look much like him, being African American, his hairstyle was different, he didn't wear a suit, and his teeth were brown, but it was the way he talked, like he wanted to make every word he said funny, only...Flitch wasn't that good at it.

"I like you, kid, and that's saying something, as I'm an ex-army ranger. I was trained, and then fired the first week." Flitch said with a laugh. "Still have the experience though, that's good. What's your name?" He sounded like a hip-hop star.

"Sam, and you are... Fli—"

"I'm Flitch. We're gonna have so much fun together! I'll be telling knock-knock jokes, and Chuck Norris jokes, while we're shooting down bad guys, and—"

He kept like this for a couple minutes, at least. In the corner of my eye I could see Thep shaking his head and rolling his eyes. Finally, Thep stopped him.

"Okay, Flitch. You can tell your Yo' Momma jokes later. I'm beginning to regret allowing you on the team. Don't make me do that. If you weren't so darn necessary, I'd fire you. But Sam here needs you. *I* need you. The *Dreamers* need you, and

Oliver Dahl

more than that, the *entire world* needs you." Thep stared sternly at Flitch.

"I understand," Flitch said, sighing sadly.

"All right then. Let's go."

"Go?" Flitch asked, incredulously.

"But I didn't bring my 'pod! Man, you should've told me it was my turn to save the world. I just downloaded this new song, and I'm not even sick of it yet! Maybe I could download *one* more? That'd keep me entertained for a good forty minutes!"

Thep groaned and I found myself biting my lip to keep from smiling.

"C'mon, Thep, can't I just wake up, grab my iPod, and fall back asleep again, and return here?

"I could get my joke book, too! I'd be real fast, I've almost mastered your sleeping skills, please, Thep?"

His shoulder's slumped. "No, Flitch. We have to get moving, now.

"All right then." Flitch agreed reluctantly, muttering under his breath about some pop star.

Thep spoke now. "All right, Sam. You ready? Grab my arm." I did, and instantly the same terribly exhilarating feeling overwhelmed me. I didn't want to have to do that again. (I hated roller coasters in the first place; cause I didn't like not being in control, but this was crazy!)

The Dreamers

Mercifully, it stopped. I looked around at my surroundings. In the horizon, I could see Future-con, all fair game.

Oliver Dahl

Chapter 8

The city seemed to focus on three colors, the primary ones: red, yellow, and blue. Tall skyscrapers did seem to actually brush the sky. Futurecon also seemed to concentrate on very fluid and round lines. Hardly anywhere in sight could I see anything entirely straight.

"Oops, sorry. I dropped us just outside of the city. I'll change that." Thep said. "Grab my arm again."

We both did, and instantly found ourselves on a sidewalk in the middle of the city!

If I'd thought the city was cool before, it was even better up close. Everything was so amazing... right down to the sidewalks!

They were a recurring pattern of yellow, blue, and red, on and on. Each sidewalk block appeared to be made out of glass, but glowed its respective primary color as if it were a TV. Maybe each sidewalk block *was* a TV... that only played

The Dreamers

red, yellow, and blue. The sidewalks alone were like New York City at night! I was astounded—I would love to live here.

The buildings were similar. The first floor was red. Moving up, the second floor would be yellow, another floor up, blue. The building repeated this pattern up and up. Each floor was a complete window, but the windows were what colored the buildings red, yellow, and blue. It was amazing! I couldn't believe the beauty and complete wackiness of it all. It was stunning.

There were two different styles of buildings. One was a normal skyscraper, but the top floor was about two or three times larger than the bottom floors, and was rounded smoothly.

The other type was especially interesting. They were pretty much floating pods the size of several football fields put together. And...they just hovered there. This led me to believe that they had transporters, or other fancy transporting gizmos.

We were standing in front of what appeared to be the largest building around. It had a very thin base, then a huge pod balanced perfectly on top, then a thin part on top, and another huge pod, and another thin part, and on and on until there were four pods. On the very top I could see a white and light-blue flag with a "D" on it. Evidently, we had a flag.

Oliver Dahl

The thin pods that the larger ones were balanced on were the size of my house! The larger pods maybe a little smaller than my loop in the neighborhood.

"We have *another* base? I thought we only had a couple hundred Dreamers or so... and that was in HQ, we have *another* one?" I asked, pointing to the flag on top of the building.

"Oh, no, no." Thep replied, shaking his head. "The flag just shows that this area of the Dream Realm is under our possession. We don't rule the place or anything, it just shows that... it's not Malfix's." Thep finished. I nodded with satisfaction.

All of the sudden the ground shook, and I knew it was a subway.

Once, I had gone with my grandparents to New York City, and I had felt the tremors of the subway below. This felt just like it.

It seemed strange that such an advanced city would still have a subway. I'd have thought they would have hovercrafts, and, well, if you had the ability to transport, you wouldn't need it... right?

Oh... well, speaking of hovercrafts, the previous thought can be scratched out, as I saw several of them now, driving across the road in front of me

They were round, like a Volkswagen Beetle,

The Dreamers

and, sure enough, floated about a foot off the ground. My childish instincts begged to ride on one, but I managed to refuse the impulse to shove a lady out of hers and go for a cruise. Oh well. Saving the world can't be all fun and games, can it?

"Enough sight seeing," Thep said, eying Flitch and I, who both stared boggle-eyed at the city.

He turned and looked at a large building far behind us. It reminded me of the Colosseum, in Rome, but more futuristic.

"That's where we need to go." Thep said, pointing.

"Why? How do you know?" Flitch asked, frowning.

Thep looked surprised at the question. "I have a hunch," he said simply.

We walked through the city, like true tourists. I loved it. It smelled fresh and clean, and perfect. We continued for a little while until we arrived at the city limits. It was very sudden. It was like... buildings, buildings, nothing.

Well, nothing wasn't right. There was a lot of stuff. By stuff, I mean roads. And bridges. And tunnels. All that stuff that makes you want to floor the gas pedal and go as fast as you can, like that one time when my dad let me drive on the way to.... Sorry, long story.

But anyway, roads were overhead, under head, side head, and... you get it. They were everywhere! They seemed woven together. If you went on one road, you probably went under about twenty others, and were above about the same! The roads looped and spiraled, and went up and down, and started to remind me more of a plate of spaghetti than an actual road.

Flitch made a funny sign with his hand, in which he made a fist, unclenched it, and repeated the process twice. One of the longer hover crafts, about the size of a small family car swerved sideways, and the doors opened automatically.

"Sweet! Hovering taxis in a futuristic city, what could be cooler?" I exclaimed.

Thep frowned at my comment, as if I had done something wrong. I took it as a hint to shut up.

We climbed in, Thep on the far side, Flitch in the middle, and me on the opposite window seat. The taxi wasn't small, or cramped, but it wasn't spacious, either.

The doors closed, and a little doohickey popped out of the dashboard in front of Flitch. He in-serted three coins and the doohickey returned into the dashboard. A small keyboard then

The Dreamers

protruded from the dash, and he typed in a destination. The keyboard then retreated. The car began to move again, slowly gaining speed until it seemed like we could be on a freeway, (although somewhat faster). All the while, Thep and I were trying to keep our mouths closed so we wouldn't throw up, and Flitch just laughed and waved his arms in the air. I shook my head in disbelief at the guy.

Lunatic. I thought. Hey, it was true. This continued for a horrible five minutes, and then we finally reached the Colosseum place.

We now walked to the arena. I hadn't noticed before, but there were hundreds filing into the arena, like there was some sort of sporting event. We hadn't seen any people in the city itself, other than drivers.

Flitch must have thought this as well, because he asked, "Who's playing, the Yankees?" He smiled, hoping to get Thep to laugh. Of course, he didn't succeed. If anything, Thep's frown increased.

Thep was acting awfully strange. He had been the one who had suggested that we came here, but as we neared, he looked more and more nervous.

All of the other "sports fans" were going toward the main entrance, and, naturally I followed along, it was natural instinct to literally, "follow the crowd." Thep called to me.

"Sam! We need to go this way," Curious, I followed. Ahead, I could see a small door, with fancy letters above it that read, *Contestants*.

"What?" Flitch gasped. "We're playing? Why? What game? If it's soccer, then I'm no good, but if it's baseball, then you're on."

"It is neither!" Thep shouted. All three of us were silent. He glared at us for a moment, and then further sped up his brisk walk. Flitch and I almost had to run to catch up with him.

"Well then... what is it, a- a fight to the death?" I offered, smiling jokingly. I was afraid of the real answer though, and I'm afraid it showed on my face.

Thep looked at me a moment, sadly, and turned his head away. It wasn't comforting, and I had the feeling that's just what it was.

"Who-o-a! I may be an ex-army ranger, but fighting really isn't my thing. I can do it, but baseball's *my* thing—!" Flitch exclaimed.

"Shut up!" Thep shouted. Neither of us asked Thep any more questions.

We entered the door, and the second we did, "the crowd went wild."

Instantly, I was hoisted by a robotic arm, and placed in a minivan-sized... was it...? Could it

The Dreamers

be…? A UFO? I looked around for extraterrestrial life forms, but didn't find any.

That's what it looked like, but a normal UFO compared to what I was in now, would be like comparing a *broken* minivan to a brand new cherry red Ferrari…with a *chainsaw* thing going on.

My UFO was ovular, and a chain went around the belly of it like a belt. On the chain were hundreds of large saw teeth. They had crumpled bits of melted metal wedged in between them, and several of them, to my shock, were stained red. What was I supposed to do? I was afraid of what the answer was.

It was a dark, forest green, and had a low windshield, like a convertible car.

A lever and a big red button told me I had guns under my hood, too. I was kind of nervous, being in this thing. If something went wrong—I was in trouble.

"How am I supposed to drive *this* thing, I don't even have my *driver's license!*" I cursed under my breath. I looked overhead and saw my face on a huge screen in the stadium.

"Wonderful." I muttered.

In the cockpit of my…vehicle, I identified a joystick. I kept telling myself "It's okay, it's a joystick, I do this in video games all the time." To be honest, it didn't really help. I strapped on my seat belt, found a couple more weapon buttons, and took a deep breath. It didn't feel quite real that I could die, and that I probably would due to my lack of knowledge on how to drive this stupid thing.

Whatever guy said, "ignorance is bliss" is a complete moron. I looked over my shoulder and saw Flitch and Thep behind me. I was first in line. I wished I could at least see how it was done, first. I would have no such luck, however. I hoped I could figure this out, somehow.

A loud voice on the intercom interrupted my thoughts.

"Hello *Dreamers*," The voice was cruel and infused with hatred.

"Welcome to the Dome. This little contest I've devised shall determine the fate of this, the city of Futurecon. If you win, I'll back away from Futurecon. If you lose, it's mine. The contest will go as follows: Three on your team, three on mine, the first team to take out two of their three opponents, wins.

"Begin."

Even though I couldn't see him, I knew that the voice belonged to Malfix. I hadn't even met him, and I already hated him.

I pushed a green button, and miraculously, I hovered off the ground. I carefully pushed the stick

The Dreamers

forward, and I went too fast, I hit a brake and stopped suddenly. I tried again. This time I went a little further, but my movements were jerky.

I could see the opposite team smoothly coming out from the furthest end of the field. They looked like they knew what they were doing. Unlike... well, someone I knew.

I looked up on the jumbotron screen as it flashed the confident faces of the opposing team. My heart skipped a few beats when I recognized one of the faces.

Gabe.

Oliver Dahl
Chapter 9

I was stunned. I was supposed to kill my best friend? I looked back at Thep and Flitch. They looked stunned as well. Each one was looking at a different player. Apparently, I wasn't the only one forced to fight a friend.

After a few more jerky movements, I got used to controlling the stupid machine, and I sped onto the field. Flitch and Thep followed behind me. I went to the farthest side, Flitch the middle, which left Thep on the opposite side.

To my dread, I saw that the person across from we was Gabe.

"It's okay," Thep shouted to me, though he sounded kind of doubtful, "This is their dream. They are simply dreaming people, and they won't get hurt if we "kill" them. They'll just wake up, understand?"

I nodded and wet my lips once more. I leaned back in my seat, my eyes looking at the trigger for my gun.

The Dreamers

I had to take a glance at Gabe. It sure didn't look like he was in a dream. He was wearing a black and neon-green suit, like the men we were supposed to be looking for. He had a smug grin on his face, like he knew he was going to crush us, and wouldn't think twice about taking all three of us out, instead of just the mandatory two.

A large force field appeared around us. We were probably twenty to thirty feet apart from each other. We were also about forty to fifty feet away from our teammates.

Gabe stretched his shoulders, and spat off the side of the... hovercraft thing. His was a dark red.

I suddenly felt foolish, looking at colors of all things, so I looked at my buddies'. Theirs were the ones I *didn't* want to shoot at.

So I turned to look at Flitch's. His was a midnight-blue color. Thep's was an ugly yellow color. We all had saws around the equator of the hovercrafts. I could see under the enemy's hoods that each of theirs had guns underneath, too.

In mine, a small screen mounted to the dashboard flickered on again, and I could see Malfix's ugly face. He had white and black hair, like Cruella De Vil, which is what stood out to me the most at first. He had pale skin and a sort of stretched face. His eyes were as red as Gabe's hovercraft and gleamed like a bloodstained sword. I shivered.

"Let the games begin. —Oh, and Dreamers, I thought you'd want to know. This is the first trial of three. You must win two out of three to remain in control. Same goes for me, but opposite!" Malfix smiled knowingly. If you end up losing, and only one of you is left, you are welcome to use replacement people, as am I." Man, this guy's smile was *wicked!* It was haunting. He talked of "replacement people" as if they were replacement *parts!*

"Start your engines!" Malfix shouted into the microphone. "Oops, sorry, they're already on..." He muttered. I almost laughed.

"Oh, forget the drama, just kill each other!" Malfix screamed, all of the sudden in a rage. It scared both teams into action.

I quickly pushed the red button on my trigger, and lasers flew out from under my hood in pairs, quick little flashes of blue light. I was aiming slightly to my left, so I missed Gabe. I didn't want to hit him, yet he was my primary target. The dirt where the lasers actually hit was singed black.

The next closest target to Gabe was to my left, so I turned and fired at Flitch's opponent. He activated a force field, and the lasers rebound-ed

The Dreamers

off the rounded surface into the sky. I had been close.

The crowd gave out a long "O-o-o-oh" Like they were disappointed that he had blocked my shot.

Idiot! I berated myself.

They were cheering for us because they didn't want Malfix to take control of their city. Of course! That would be good to know. I was learning all sorts of stuff. I hoped I would be able to use that information later on.

I turned my gun back to Gabe and was about to fire, but I had to quickly duck to avoid his lasers going over me. They didn't stop. My neck began to cramp. I searched for a button that read "force-field". I couldn't find it, but waited. I drove my hovercraft higher. Gabe continued to shoot at me. It would only be a matter of seconds until his lasers would catch up.

"Perfect." I muttered grumpily. I imagined a force field appearing around my hovercraft. Nothing happened. I imagined the enemy's craft growing a force field and took that clip and applied it to mine. Gabe's enemy's faded. *Zoop!* I now had a force-field. I'd done it! I don't know *how* I'd done it, but I got several strange looks, anyway. The looks scared me. They said, "you're not supposed to be able to do that." At the moment, I didn't care.

Oliver Dahl

Unable to react fast enough, Gabe's lasers bounced off of my force field and hit him, square in the chest. The force threw him out of his IFO and he fell twenty feet to the ground. I couldn't bear to see him hurt like that, but I knew I'd done the right thing. I muttered an apology.

As if something miraculous had occurred, Gabe's ship exploded, and a part of it rebounded off Flitch's opponent's head. I heard him swear and then pick the piece up and chuck it at Flitch. Flitch quickly swerved to avoid it, then tried opening fire, now that his opponent's force field was gone.

Flitch's lasers grazed his enemy on the arm before he could get it started up again.

Even from this distance, I could tell that it had singed through his jumpsuit and went through some of his arm; I could see the blood. I could faintly hear the guy yell in pain. My eyes watered in sympathy for my enemy. That *must* have hurt. A lot.

I carefully drove my IFO around the enemy side and back around to where Thep was fighting some other old guy.

"Need help?" I shouted.

Thep's foe heard me too, and quickly turned and fired at me—all in one fluid movement. He was watching smoothly as the projectile flew towards me.

The Dreamers

"Whoa!" I shouted in alarm.

I put my hovercraft into a dive and then swerved to avoid...a bomb that was dropped by the third hovercraft.

"Not fair!" I complained, searching for my "bomb" button. I found it; it was fair after all. I flew up high and aligned myself above the enemy, checking to see that Flitch was okay. My shock made me push the button, and the bomb nearly hit Thep! He started listing off a few choice swearwords at me, but I ignored him, pointing in Flitch's direction, trying to get him to understand. I could only hope that he did.

Somehow, his opponent had obliterated his hovercraft, so it lay up side down on the dirt floor of the arena. I couldn't see Flitch, but I expected he was dead, as the scoreboard on the screen read:

Dreamers: 1
Malfix: 1

I hadn't known Flitch very long, but it was heart breaking to think of someone with such a sense of humor, (even if it was lousy) dead.

I took another deep breath and tried not to cry. I once again tried to line myself up on top of Thep's opponent. I wasn't sure if I could do it, pull the trigger, I mean, but for now, I just tried to line myself up.

It was nearly impossible! Thep's friend/enemy was moving around like a wasp; hovering a second or two, and moving, hovering, moving. He was nearly impossible to get to! Whenever I fired, he was already well out of the way of the lasers.

Instead, I decided to try avenging Flitch by going after *his* attacker. He was a little easier. I pushed the bomb button. The bomb made contact and blew a large chunk of the back off his hovercraft. Losing control, he fell in the damaged vehicle twenty feet to the arena floor and exploded on contact. It was easy to tell that the driver had woken up from this nightmare.

We had done it!
We had won!

The Dreamers
Chapter 10

We had no time to celebrate. There were two other contests. "Oh yeah, the other two contests," You may be thinking. In my mind, I was thinking something more along the lines of, "Oh crap! Two more chances for me to die a painful death at the hands of people who are really asleep!"

So yeah, you could pretty much say I was bummed. But there were two good bits of news. One, of course, we had won! And the other, much more important, Flitch had only been injured under the IFO, not killed. It seemed too perfect—too much of a living cliche! Of course, he had been scratched up pretty bad, and he could hardly stand, but Thep and I were glad he was alive. (Even if he did have a pretty bad sense of humor.)

And so, being Flitch, the first words he spoke to us were, "Knock-knock!"

I followed along with the joke and it ended up being that stupid one about owls. (Knock-knock, who's there? Who? Who who?, Hey, did I hear an owl?" That one). My sister has nearly driven me insane before, using that one. Just thinking about it makes me homesick.

Malfix's angry voice boomed over the arena once again.

"And now for round two. A simple car race. There are no rules. Survival is the prize."

We wouldn't hear from him again for a while.

Robotic hands grabbed us again and I began to fear what the "simple car race" actually was. I had driven go-carts at amusement parks and stuff, but I doubted these were little bumper cars connected to the ceiling with a pole.

I soon found that my beliefs were correct. I'll describe it to you.

It was a car, that's for sure. A very fancy one. Mine was a golden color, painted with shimmering scales like a dragon's. A big, shining engine protruded out of the front hood.

Once again, the glass was very thin, as if the creators wanted as little protection for me as possible.

But my tires were pretty awesome. From the side, they looked like normal wheels. But at a diagonal view, you could see that spikes could be deployed.

There was also a large weapon of some sort,

The Dreamers

carefully concealed under my hood. That was freaky.

The robotic arm lifted me up and put me in the front seat of the hot rod. I now knew that it was a good idea to know what weapons you had.

Oil slick... spiked tires... saltate (whatever that was!)... Flame-thrower... ejector seat.... This was beginning to remind me of Speed Racer! After I saw that I also had tacks, rockets, and a booster engine, (I might as well have had "Death by Platypuses") a larger robotic arm picked up and carried my car to the starting line. The racetrack seemed to have come out of the ground of the stadium, like the stadium was a giant, 3D printer.

"How do you win?" I asked Thep, who was coming my way via robotic arm.

"We must get two of our three players in the top three." He said simply.

I decided that he knew too much, and was withholding some information from Flitch and I.

On this round, Thep had a pretty good vehicle. His had a huge robotic arm, like the one that just dropped him off, attached to the back of his car. It was rounded, like an oval, and looked like it might have been a recycled hovercraft.

And this time, Flitch got the best car. His was dark purple, and was more a monster truck than a hot rod. It had huge rockets on either side,

Oliver Dahl

and looked like it could crush all of the other cars in one rotation of the tire!

"Hey guys! Could you imagine me "knock-knocking" doors in this baby? They wouldn't ask any questions!" Flitch laughed maniacally and returned his head back into his monster truck. I shook my head incredulously.

Well, the race would be easy for him. Floor the gas for two seconds, and he would be at the finish line.

"Start your engines!" Came the cry of a chubby official. Even the vertical black and white stripes of his uniform couldn't hide the guy's fat.

I pressed a green button and a loud roar carried on over the course. I realized with a shock that it was my car, and that I had just gotten everyone's attention.

Oh great, now I'm a target, I groaned inwardly.

"Three!" Came the shout of the official. Everyone revved his or her engine.

"Two!" The smell of exhaust filled the air.

"One!" The ref said, obviously ready to say the last word, the word that would send us off.

"Go!" He yelled, waving a green flag.

I punched the gas and took my foot off the brake. I may not have had my driver's license, but this felt pretty natural. I swung the steering wheel

The Dreamers

to my left, and I turned left so smoothly, I couldn't believe it. I followed that turn around, then briskly turned right and up. Ahead, Flitch was shouting like a maniac. One of our fellow racers shot a heat-seeking missile at him, but with one quick turn, the projectile went too far ahead, and nearly blew up the scoreboard!

I was going up an incline, and the road was separating in the middle, like a bridge over a river, when they need to let a boat through. I groaned again, and decided that I would have to jump.

I pushed on the gas pedal even harder, and I sped up the side of the bridge. It was at a forty five-degree angle now, and quickly nearing ninety.

Somehow I managed to push the poor pedal harder. I zoomed almost straight up the bridge and for a moment, I was suspended in air.

My car twisted around three hundred sixty degrees—vertically, then I twisted and landed on the opposite side! It seemed to have happened in slow motion. I again got the look from the audience and fellow contestants. They stared at me like I'd done something amazing—impossible even. I again ignored it, though I knew that I had!

I hit the ground harder than I would have liked, but quickly regained control and glued my foot to the gas. I was off!

The other people would have to wait for the

bridge to close again! Thanks to my stunt, our team had gained a huge advantage. Hopefully Flitch had gotten to the finish line by now. I looked at the scoreboard and saw that he hadn't. *Oh well,* I thought, *it was too much to ask for.* All of the sudden, a large car with a scorpion-like theme zoomed ahead of me. So much for that advantage. I found my rocket button and pushed it desperately.

A small rocket about the length of a small school desk in size popped out of my car's hood and flew to the scorpion car. The missile slowed down behind it, and then sped up and hit the car, just as I was side to side with it.

Green flames twirled out of the car at a ferocious speed. I yanked the wheel to the right to avoid being pushed off the track. I could hear the audience cheering. The paint on the side of my car bubbled and fizzed.

I swerved to get back in the middle of the road, and tried to go as fast as I could. I didn't think I had reached maximum, yet. I was almost afraid to find out!

Another car, decorated with purple and pink flames zoomed ahead before I could do anything about it.

A minute later, the scoreboard read a familiar score:

The Dreamers

Dreamers: 1
Malfix: 1

Another car—this one a dull, rusty red—passed me. How many of the cars were Malfix's? Way more than the three of us Dreamers. Malfix had again cheated.

I continued to floor the gas, until it just seemed like that's how driving worked. For the heck of it, I dumped tacks and oil slick all over the road.

I could see the finish the line, and as I looked to my side, the red car's driver's face was fixed on the line, too. I could hear someone behind me, flailing on my traps. I looked in my mirror and saw...Thep! He quickly got over my traps and picked my car up.

"Whoa! Thep! I'm sorry! I didn't know that you were right behind—" My apologies were lost in the wind as Thep used his robotic arm and threw my car with great accuracy over a sea of enemy cars, missiles, traps, and other things that exploded. My car spun like when I jumped the bridge, but worse, like transporting with Thep. (Don't tell him I said that, that would only make him angrier!)

I finally landed, somehow on all four tires, behind the finish line. I looked at the scoreboard, and my heart sunk like a boulder through water. We had lost.

Dreamers: 2
Malfix: 3

"Driving must not be your forte," came a voice we all knew was Malfix's. Thep pulled past the finish line, spitting dirt from his mouth as he exited the car, and walked toward me.

The enemy drivers exchanged high-fives and fist-bumps, laughing as they did it.

"You should hope that you're good at mazes, Dreamers." Malfix chuckled. He left us with haunting words.

"Last game... *last* game."

The Dreamers
Chapter 11

Last game. It *was* the last game. Why couldn't it just be rock, paper, scissors, two for three? I could imagine Flitch asking Malfix, "How about three for five?"

Since Malfix's eerie parting words, Thep had figured out the guy's foreshadowing.

"I bet he puts us in the Labyrinth." he complained.

"What's the Labyrinth?" Flitch asked.

Thep looked at me. I shrugged and said. "Hey, *I* don't want to know."

He then turned to Flitch and replied, "A maze. A horrific maze of nightmares usually used to torture enemies of the council of Futurecon. There's a fifty-fifty chance that we come out alive."

"What do we need to accomplish?"

"We need to get to the other end of the maze without dying. In this case, I think that all three of us need to get to the end. It could be a variation of some sort, though. So if one of us dies, we'd better hope that somebody on their team does, too. Because if they don't, Futurecon will be under Malfix's control. Futurecon is much too valuable to let Malfix control it. With Futurecon under his boot, he could very easily gain control of the other territories.

Once again, and suddenly, robotic arms picked us up and brought us over to a long table. To my horror I found that it was covered in weapons.

Swords, spears, bows and arrows lined one side, on another there were rifles, pistols, and grenades.

In the center of the table were machine guns, better grenades, shruikans, even RPG's. On the closest side were pointy and other futuristic things that were either explosive, or probably emitted lasers.

"Choose your weapons." Malfix ordered. I experimentally picked up a shruikan, though I knew I wouldn't use it. I hesitated, then grabbed a little machine gun that shot tiny metal pellets, like a BB gun. I had no doubt that it would do much more damage, however, than a BB gun.

Flitch looked at me incredulously, holding up a squirt gun and a water balloon.

The Dreamers

"Really?" He asked, grinning despite the circumstances.

I laughed along with him.

Thep approached us.

"Going with the heavy artillery, are you?" He asked, shouldering a light rifle after testing the weight and grabbing ammunition. I hoped he was good with rifles.

"Are you kidding?" Flitch asked.

"No, the latex in those water balloons releases an electric current of at least twenty amps when it is wet and exposed to air. The water is full of bits of copper, if you hit someone with it, they will be over-cooked."

"Same with the squirt gun, then?" Flitch asked, his smile gone.

"Pretty much." Thep replied.

"Okay, then. I'll take these!" Flitch said, laughing again.

"No surprise there," Thep muttered.

We turned to sneak a peak at what our opponents had selected. One had loaded himself up with knives. Another had a large machine gun strapped to his back. The other held two automatic pistols, and had a laser gun tucked into his belt.

Compared to water balloons and a squirt gun, I decided we had a slight disadvantage when it came to weapons.

Oliver Dahl

I decided that this was getting much too serious, and a little too dangerous. I didn't want to do this. I wished this were a dre—oh, right. Darn. It was. Maybe I could wake myself up.

Wake up! I thought. I was feeling selfish enough to let Thep and Flitch do this on their own! I never asked to be a Dreamer! I never asked to save the world! I never asked to be slaughtered in a maze by some sleepwalking guy with a machine gun! Imagine *that* for a gravestone marker! "Here lies Sam Kullen, killed by a sleep-walking"— never mind

"Wake up!" I urged myself. It didn't work. It looked as if I'd have to work this one out.

Once again, the robotic arms picked us up and gently placed us down in front of an entrance where we were given instructions by Malfix over a P.A. system. While he did, I thought angrily in my mind, *Why don't you come down here and do the maze, see how you like it!*

"The rules are simple. In the maze are five golden orbs. If you touch them before the opposing team, you will be awarded points. The team with the highest score wins. Lest you think it'll be easy—the other team wants nothing more than to see you dead. If the opposing team has more living players than you do, at the end, you lose.

"Let the games begin!"

The Dreamers
Chapter 12

Hey, well, remember when I said, "In the horizon, I could see Futurecon, all fair game?" Well... it wasn't really much of a fair game at all.

We walked into the big hallway, and immediately the doors slammed shut behind us. Dimly lit light bulbs blinked on. Several of them flickered off.

Ahead, I could see a golden orb a little bigger than a baseball floating in the air. "Wow, it can't be *that* easy!" I said, pointing at it.

Flitch ran to it and touched it. We heard a "ding" outside and a cheer of fans. Seconds later, another "ding" and the crowd booed. Evidently, our opponents had found one too.

"Come on!" I encouraged. We walked down and quickly found a fork in the maze.

"That way leads to the enemy," Thep said, pointing left. " Their entrance was to the left of us. We should go this way." Thep began walking right.

Oliver Dahl

Flitch and I followed; glad we didn't have to make these kinds of decisions. We walked for perhaps five minutes or so, and reached a three-way fork. Each looked similar, and had dim, flickering light bulbs hanging the ceiling. One of which gave a violent flash and exploded! We all jumped in surprise.

"What do we do now?" Flitch asked, realizing it was just a light bulb.

Thep smiled. "I thought these might come in handy." He removed a GPS from his bag—the judges had been too stupid to check it! What luck!

"It's time to use these." Thep decided. He examined the GPS a moment.

"Alright, we need to continue this way," he said, pointing down the middle branch.

"After two hundred feet or so, we'll go left. There is one in that left hall. This GPS is made specially in Futurecon, and can identify other near objects."

We walked down the hall for a couple minutes, when I asked, "What about the other team?" We all froze.

"Oh yeah..." Flitch said, looking around nervously. The maze behind us creaked suddenly and we whirled. Nothing was there. In the distance, as if on cue, we heard a large roar. The sound echoed through the maze.

The Dreamers

Realizing that it wasn't near us, whatever it was, as it definitely wasn't the other team, we cautiously moved on. Soon thereafter, Flitch put his hand in front of me, keeping me from moving any further, and called up to Thep, "Hey Thep, what's this?" Alerted, Thep ran back, and turned to look at whatever Flitch was pointing at. He was in for a surprise.

"Fool! It's a camera! We're probably on that big screen right now!"

Laughing from outside told us he was right. Even in the darkness, we could see Flitch blushing.

"Well, you wanna hear a knock-knock joke?" He asked the camera.

The crowd laughed harder, and now we were blushing too. "C'mon Flitch, we need to hurry!"

"Oh right... sorry." Thep and I both doubted his apology was sincere, but we continued on anyway.

We quickly reached the fork, and Thep ran ahead through the left hall to see...nothing! There wasn't anything there. While the audience was laughing, we must have not heard the "ding".

"Come here," Thep ordered. Suddenly, Thep's head dropped to the ground. He seemed to be looking at something.

He carefully stood up and walked towards us. In a quiet voice, he said, "Friends, slowly unsheathe your weapons and follow me." Someone was near. I removed my machine gun and put it to my shoulder as I walked.

I looked through a handy night-vision scope on top, and thought I saw a movement.

"Behind the wall!" I shouted without thinking. *Great. Now they know where we are and that we're expecting them.* I berated myself for my stupidity.

But at least we knew where they were too, I guess. Miraculously, Flitch threw a water balloon, and it hit one of them square in the face! Arches of blue light briefly lit up the cavern from his water balloon, and sent tension through the room. Flitch's hair was standing on end slightly.

I fired at a guy who was sneaking up behind us. I hit him in the face, directly under his eye, and he dropped his pistols. I ran up to him, kicked him between the legs, and picked up his guns. I threw one back to Flitch, and finished the guy by knocking him out with the handle of the gun. He slumped to the floor, unconscious. His true body must have woken up, because he and the person that Flitch had chucked his water balloon at had disappeared.

There was one other guy, and he was much smarter. I struggled to remember what weapon he had...he had the knives!

The Dreamers

Not two seconds later, I saw a knife spinning through the air, catching and reflecting the light of the dim bulbs. Everything seemed to slow down, like the air had turned to syrup. Once again I found myself wishing this were only a dream, and remembering that it was, but in my case, that fact didn't help me. The knife continued on its path toward me, the blade spinning up and down, end over end. I tried to turn and run, but I was frozen in place. I braced myself for the inevitable impact that would soon follow.

The knife slammed home with a sickening crunch. However, I wasn't the "home!" I don't remem-ber how it happened, but a large shield seemed to have materialized at the last possible second right in front of me. The shield now had an eighteen-inch blade stuck in its surface. The shield saved my life! What just happened, and how it happened is still a mystery to me.

Flitch and Thep looked at me like I'd performed a miracle, so this only added to my confusion.

Suddenly, the syrup turned back to air and I could move again. *Thank goodness!* I thought. I quickly aimed and fired my machine gun at the hooded figure that had just thrown his knife at me. There was a quick flash of steel, and I heard the bullet bounce somewhere left of me. *Bang!* Thep had fired. No knife could have stopped the rifle bullet from less than three yards away. The bullet went all the way through the guy then ricocheted off the stone wall behind him. The poor dude turned into steam and vanished.

"Did we win?" I asked, panting. After all, the whole ordeal probably took less than a minute.

As if to answer me, Malfix's angry voice spoke over the intercom. "Well Dreamers, you have defeated my team, but you *still* must find two more orbs!"

Thep cursed.

"Well, at least I have this," He muttered, holding up his GPS. "Ha!" He laughed. "What luck! There's one to our right, too.

We backed up and turned right instead, and, sure enough, just a few yards ahead, floated a golden orb. I ran ahead and touched it. We didn't need a microphone to hear Malfix.

"Any others near?" I asked eagerly, hoping against hope for luck.

"We must have incredible luck. Luck like never before experienced!" Thep said with obvious joy in his voice. He ran ahead, leaving Flitch and I behind. We heard laughing and flash of gold light. Another "ding" and the crowd screamed and cheered once more.

"We did it, we did it!" I celebrated.

The Dreamers

All of the sudden, the maze seemed to dissolve and we were left standing in the middle of an empty arena.

We hugged each other and clapped one another on the back.

Malfix was at the microphone, hissing and spitting into it. "You won this time, *Dreamers*!" He shouted Dreamers like it was an insult.

"But it won't happen again! You haven't the seen the last of me!" Malfix disappeared, and the crowd went wild.

Chapter 13

"What's next?" I asked, hoping for the best.

"The Ice Caves." Thep replied.

"Won't we need to go back to the base first?" Flitch asked.

Thep simply shook his head in reply. "I don't think so. But we need to get out of here.

"What I want to know," Flitch said, "Is how you knew that this was where we needed to go."

"I could sense Malfix's presence. There is something in a Dreamer's imagination that makes them easy to sense. That's how I, and others like me, can immediately find new Dreamers. I knew that Sam was in the jungle, I could feel his presence." Thep replied simply.

That's another thing I liked about Thep. All of his answers were simple, and didn't state the obvious—most of the time. As we walked out of the arena, I decided it was my turn to ask a question. It had been on my mind for a while now,

The Dreamers

and I was very eager to know the answer. I licked my lips in preparation.

"How did Edmund Huntle, and the rest of the Dreamer leaders make the Titanic sink, and all of that stuff?"

"Aah. Finally. A good question." Thep said. "Basically, there are two types of Dreams. One, is this one. The type that we are in now. Where our bodies physically trade places with our shadows and we can live and breathe in the Dream Realm.

"The other kind is special. You can use it to control things on earth, you can simply dream that a wildfire never happens, or that a planned terrorist attack goes entirely wrong.

"However, you require a Dreamer ring, which are only given to highly trusted officials. Me being one of them," Thep finished, showing a ring on his hand.

"These rings make it extremely easy to dream up these things, it anchors our mind to reality, and gives us the ability to think as we influence events."

"But then how did—?" I interrupted, or at least, *tried* to interrupt.

"Patience. The rings were developed over a long period of trials, most resulting in failure. Edmund Huntle did not have a Dreamer ring, so he could not control his dreams nearly as easily.

That's why the *Titanic* went down, and all those other accidents.

"However, we are rarely the sole cause of such accidents. Edmund may have dreamed that an iceberg simply formed in front of the *Titanic*, that's all. Sometimes, all we do is dream of some-body, and they get dark ideas from us. That's where some terrorism cases came from.

"What other things have been caused by Dreamers?" I asked curiously.

"Since you haven't had a chance to read through the handbook yet, I'll tell you a few.

"It says that 'political assassinations, the invention of the mobile phone, landing on the moon, the stock market crash leading to the great depression,' a great number more." Thep offered.

"Are there any other events like that? And, if the Dreamers are the good guys, then why are we assassinating world leaders and stuff?"

"Good questions! Oh, sure!" Thep said. "Most inventions, and, contrary to popular belief, it was actually a Dreamer (though before the cult was actually founded) that caused the Chicago fire of 1871, not a cow.

"This deals with your last question, about killing leaders and market crashes, those accidents. They are not intended in the slightest, and if Dreamer rings had been created and used then,

The Dreamers

none of those things would have happened." Thep replied sadly.

"Wait, but if you can control your dreams and make your dreams come true and real, then...couldn't you have just dreamed that we would win Malfix's little contests?" Flitch asked. He had a point. I too, gazed at Thep, quizzically, expecting an answer.

"No, unfortunately you cannot use Dreamer Rings to bring about things in the Dream Realm. Otherwise Malfix would have been dealt with long ago. It is complicated."

"What about Malfix?"

"His ability to manipulate other people's dreams—to control them continues to grow, and unfortunately, he uses those powers for his own selfish desires.

We traveled in silence until we reached the door of the arena. We walked down the steps until the cement leveled out, and we could see Future-con and the road that took us here.

Thep didn't have to tell us to grab his arm. We knew the drill.

Instantly, we were off, spinning through space.

Chapter 14

We arrived, or more like, crash-landed in an arctic wasteland.

Icy cold, surrounded in ice, white with ice and snow. Why did it have to be here? Why couldn't it be in that Paradisa place? Oh well, I guess saving the world can't *always* be fun and games.

Anyway, I was glad we were one down two to go. But as you will be able to attest in a few lines, ("bear" with me) I was not glad to be here.

Here's why. Giant polar bears. Yup. We had landed less than a hundred yards from two giant polar bears. About twenty feet high on their hind legs, and about as long as a bus. Exaggerating? Maybe a little. But they *were* huge.

Their fur was a dirty, yellowish white, and their muzzles looked like they were covered in blood. Two seal/narwhal things lay gutted beside them. The bears must have decided that we looked

The Dreamers

tastier, or something, because they came running after us.

Still sore from my little marathon in the jungle, running was painful. Not only were my muscles screaming in agony, but I was sure I had at least half a dozen blisters on my feet!

"This way!" Thep shouted, taking off. We ran after him for all we were worth, not knowing or really caring why this direction was better than any other.

The polar bears were gaining on us. Thep began to lag behind and Flitch went ahead. The deep snow made it hard to run. My face felt red, and breathing was painful.

Wishing we were close enough to grab Thep's arm, I pounded onward, ignoring the pain, ignoring how blissful "transporting" with Thep would be compared to this.

I felt like an Indian chief sending off smoke signals, with as much steam was coming out of my mouth as there was. (Yeah, okay, I guess I'm exaggerating again...)

The bears were closer. Their breathy grunts were getting louder. The sound reminded me of when I was being chased in the jungle. Was that just last night? It seemed like it was weeks ago!

As much as I hated Mrs. Trell's math class, for the first time in my life, I thought I might rather

Oliver Dahl

be there than here! For a moment I couldn't believe I'd thought that, but then, looking back, knew I was being truthful.

We continued to run, hoping that the bears would lose interest, give up, and go back to their seal dinner. Why were they chasing us? They had seal already!

Risking a glance back, I realized I'd miscounted. Did I say two of them? Now there were four within fifty yards of us, but then dozens more trailing behind them.

"The farther we run, the more of them there are!" I complained, panting.

I thought I heard someone call my name. I shook my head and ignored it. Ignored *it* along with my aching muscles, burning lungs, and blisters.

Flitch suddenly turned around, the laser gun that he'd been issued at HQ in his hands. He fired several lasers at the lead bear. The big bear dropped and slid to a stop, snow piling up in front of him like a snowplow. The other bears crowded around him, unsure perhaps of what exactly had happened. Fortunately, it distracted them long enough to put another forty or fifty yards between us.

Ahead, I could see a large mountain that hadn't been there before.

The Dreamers

It looked like a giant slab of ice, an *enormous* slab of ice. The thing was gigantic! Maybe not the size of a mountain, but definitely a very tall hill. Thep told us what it was. "The Ice Caves!"

From where we were, if you squinted, you could see little pockmarks in the mountain.

The closer we got, the bigger and easier it was to identify the caves. Each cave was fairly small; the largest of which was maybe the size of a small family room. The smallest was much less in size.

Out of nowhere, I could hear light laughter. It sounded like it was coming from behind me. No, to my right. No—now right above me! I looked around but saw nothing! I felt something jab my side, but nothing was there. It sounded like...like my sister!

I could still hear Cynthia talking "Sam? Sam? Are you 'wake?" All of my surroundings melted and my eyes opened suddenly, startling Cynthia.

"Oh!" She screamed, holding her hands close to her chest. "You *are* 'wake!" She squealed. She jumped on my bed and started hugging me. As annoying as this was, it was much better than being eaten by giant polar bears.

With a start I looked at my alarm clock.

5:12! I doubted that it was AM time. I couldn't believe it!

"Oh man!" I anguished. "I've been asleep for..." I did some quick subtraction, "Ten hours! Plus last night! That's... twenty hours!"

I jumped off my bed, again not bothering to make it, and ran downstairs.

My mother looked at me, concerned.

"Hey Sam," She said soothingly. "How'd you sleep?"

It took me a while to get the joke. "Oh... oh, right. Um..." I racked my brain for an excuse. Then I remembered. *Of course!*

"I dunno. I guess that cold kind of wore me out." I shrugged like it wasn't a big deal. She looked at me like, W*hat is going on with you?*

She then sighed and the expression went away.

"How do you feel now, Honey?"

"Much better, thanks, Mom."

"Where are you going?" She asked curiously, watching me head back up to my room. I couldn't exactly tell her "Back to bed, Mom." Let alone, "Back to save the world."

My mouth moved with my thoughts until I came up with another excuse.

"Ah... bathroom."

"Oh, of course, it's been, what? Twenty

The Dreamers

hours? Fifteen? Something like that." She then sighed and shook her head in a worrying expression.

"Yeah," I headed back upstairs, I *did* need to go to the bathroom.

After that, I couldn't decide what to do. I felt like I'd just been... just been chased by a bunch of polar bears on an alien world. I was psyched, and there was no way I could fall asleep like *this*.

Of course, I thought I could knock myself unconscious with something hard, but that probably wouldn't be a good idea. What I needed was sleeping gas. Unfortunately, I doubted there was a sleeping gas store in my neighborhood.

Back in my room, I began to pace. I lay down on my bed, trying to meditate: no good. I had too much to think about. I pulled out my notebook and scribbled down my thoughts. I've found that this helps clear my mind. This is what I wrote.

1. Thep and Flitch are alone.
2. Polar bears may have caught them.
3. Hopefully they are still alive.
4. I don't know how to fall asleep

Oliver Dahl

I put down a couple more, but these are the important ones. I needed to get back with Thep and Flitch! At least just know if they were alive! It was kind of weird thinking that if I didn't fall asleep, lives might be at risk.

I thought and thought of anything that came to mind about sleeping. Still, nothing came. And then I had it.

I needed to eat lots of candy, get a good sugar buzz, and then I'd crash. If it worked on You-Tube, it'd work on me.

No way my mom would let me have a bunch of candy. I mean, I have a "cold," right? I'd have to sneak it, somehow.

I smelled lunch cooking. And then I smelled a plan.

The Dreamers
Chapter 15

Every Halloween, when my sister and I trick-or-treated (yes, I *do* trick-or-treat, [and will until the end of life!]) and every Easter, we put all our candy in our own bucket. Add to that a couple parades during the summer, and we get enough candy to last almost all year long, if you only eat a piece or two per day. We call them our "treat buckets."

I am pretty smart, and only eat a treat or two occasionally, so that when Easter and Halloween roll around, I still have candy. At the moment we had quite a few after a family reunion. Unfortunately, though, some of it gets pretty stale.

I came downstairs and saw my mom cooking spaghetti noodles. I pretended to walk like it was tiring, and I was sore. (Which I was, so it wasn't hard.)

"Hey Mom, I'm expecting a new art catalog in the mail." I coughed, and pretended to swallow.

"Could you go check the mail for me? I still don't feel, too well."

She looked at me curiously. I was afraid she'd see through this whole thing, but then she replied. "Sure, honey," and went outside to get it. I didn't like lying, but I guessed if the fate of the world depended on it....

I looked over my shoulder to see that she had closed the door, and I quickly opened the cupboard door above the microwave and grabbed my treat bucket.

I then ran upstairs and put it under my bed. I came back downstairs and was pretending to stir the spaghetti noodles when my mom came back in again.

"Was it there?" I asked, pretending to sound eager.

"No. But it looks like Gabe put something in the mail for you. Dunno why, he sees you at school every day, plus, you two text all the time."

My heart skipped a beat. I'd nearly forgotten about Gabe.

"Oh, thanks, Mom!" I said, running up to my room with the letter. I decided to read first, then eat the candy. I opened the envelope and unfolded the paper inside. It was on a piece of folded (and stained) notebook paper. The handwriting was messy, but I could make it out.

The Dreamers

Hey, Sam. It's me, Gabe. I decided that this was a little to weird and embarrassing to tell you face-to-face. I'm a wimp like that. You see, last night I had a weird dream. It felt so real, and vivid, that I just sat up and thought about it in bed. It was too serious for me to just text you, plus I can't find my phone. It is kind of embarrassing, but....

I dreamed that we like, fought in these hovercraft things, and we had to kill each other in them!

I know, I know, it's stupid, but like I ~~said~~ wrote before, it was so vivid and real, I could feel the steering wheel in my hands... but more than that, I felt the pain from each blow! I dunno. It just seemed like it actually happened. I don't know why I'm telling you this, sorry if it sounds stupid. Oh well, that's me.

Gabe

I was stunned. I didn't know what to think. Gabe had remembered the dream! Was *he* a Dreamer too?

I didn't think so. Gabe was just too... Gabe! He didn't have an imagination! I decided to text him back, so that when he found his phone, he could read it. I privately hoped he wouldn't find it for a *long* time. I can't remember exactly what I wrote, but it was something like: "Gabe, interesting dream... That is pretty silly. What kind of movies have you been watching that inspired *that* dream? I think you need to lay off the doughnuts!"

I felt bad lying. Not only to Gabe, but also to my mother.

Pushing my feelings aside, I grabbed my treat bucket from under my bed and began opening all of the chocolate stuff first.

Fun-size Snickers, Butterfingers, Milky Ways, Reese's, Twix bars, they all went down my throat.

After a while, the chocolate began to taste bitter. I popped a Toxic Waste in my mouth, but had to spit it out, it was so sour after all that chocolate.

I ate some candy canes from Christmas, some left over jellybeans from Easter, and other miscellaneous stuff.

I downed at least four Pixie Stix, three Fun-Dips, and somehow managed to swallow two jolly ranchers.

Finally, I couldn't eat any more, and so I stopped. After about ten minutes, my fingers began to twitch. A few minutes following that, my hands

The Dreamers

began to shake so bad, I could barely hold on to a pencil!

My eyebrows twitched and I couldn't seem to hold still. I found myself bouncing in my chair.

Soon I couldn't take it anymore. I stood on my bed and jumped like a crazed monkey.

Thinking back on that moment, I realize I must have looked like I belonged in an asylum, with chocolate and artificial colorings smeared on my face, jumping on my bed.

I wiped the stuff off my face, and went down to lunch, giggling slightly. I quickly ate my spaghetti—which tasted *horrid* after all that sweet stuff. While I was eating, my feet were practically dancing under the table.

I then flew back up to my room, bounced on my bed some more, and then finally lied down.

Suddenly, the energy inside of me disappeared and I slumped on my bed. I pretty much collapsed. Satisfied, I tucked myself in and entered Dreamland once more. I was ready to save my friends, and the world, all in an afternoon nap.

Chapter 16

I awoke in a—no, that's not quite right. It's hard to explain. I sort of awoke, I guess, but it was in a dream. I dunno. Unless you've skipped all the way to chapter sixteen, you know what I mean.

Well, anyway, I awoke in what must be an ice cave. Across to my right, more to the back of the cave—crevice, really, was Flitch and Thep.

Flitch was the first to speak. "You freaked us out! One moment you're running right behind me, the next you're gone. We almost went back and zapped some bears thinking one of them got you."

"We figured you must have awoken. You dreamed yourself into our cave, and there are hundreds you could have gone into. You're definitely getting the hang of waking up in the right place." he commented.

"I dunno. I just fell asleep—which wasn't easy—and woke up, well, showed up, here." I replied.

The Dreamers

"Well, I came up with a new knock-knock joke. Do you wanna hear it?" Flitch asked.

"If it pertains to polar bears in any way whatsoever, no." I replied. I could tell Thep was thinking those exact words. Flitch looked pretty disappointed, but hey, there was a time and a place for knock-knock jokes. This wasn't one of them.

The cave appeared to be about twelve feet deep, and after looking around, I noticed the entrance was twenty feet high off the ground.

"How did you get up here?" I asked curiously.

"Thep did some Dreamer magic...." Flitch replied mysteriously.

I turned to Thep with a questioning look on my face. He nodded grudgingly.

"Whatever. What do we do now?" I asked.

"Watch. This is pretty awesome!" Flitch said.

He pressed lightly on the back of the cave wall and a small segment opened like a door on a hinge. "Tah dah!" He finished, waving his arms dramatically at the hole.

"So... what are we waiting for?"

Thep took this one. "I need to rest. That run completely wore me out. I'm getting too old for this."

We waited in silence for a while in that cave.

Oliver Dahl

Out of pure curiosity, I asked, "How long was I gone? Away from you guys, I mean."

"Oh, perhaps a couple hours or so..." Thep said. A couple hours! I was barely awake for two! I was sure that Thep had another "it's complicated" answer, but I asked anyway.

"Does time go faster in the Dream Realm than on earth?"

"Yes, just under two times, in fact."

"Oh." was all I could say. That was an interesting fact to know.

After a couple moments, Thep said he was ready, and managed to stand up, (with the help of Flitch and I). After that, he was fine.

Flitch crawled through the hole first. Thep went next, and then me. When I got through, I was amazed at what I saw.

A perfect spiral staircase carved entirely out of ice went up and down for nearly as far as I could see. It glittered and shone, and there was no need for light, because even the smallest bit of sunlight that went through the secret doors shone ten times the light on the staircase.

"Wow..." I murmured. It echoed silently around the room.

The staircase had hundreds little icicles dangling from it. Some nearly as large as my arm, others only the size of a pencil.

The Dreamers

The whole thing shimmered a very light blue. So light, it was nearly white.

I was simply astonished at how *perfect* it was. It was a perfect helix, so perfect, I wondered if it was really made by human hands!

Clearly, Flitch, and even Thep were impressed.

"It's beautiful." Thep commented. Flitch and I could only nod.

"So... we climb it then?" Flitch asked.

"All the way to the top." Thep replied.

I sighed. This might take a while.

~D~

We took the first steps. Well, obviously we didn't take the middle steps, but... you know what I mean. It was sort of painful, stepping on the staircase. It was beautiful—a true work of art. I felt like I was defiling it.

I know what you're thinking. "Sam, you're such a wimp. You're worried about a stupid staircase." Yeah, it's hard to explain. It was like... you didn't want to eat a cake because it was so well decorated! And how you wince when you see the first slice cut off... you know, kind of like that, I guess.

It was strange. The higher we climbed, the

warmer it seemed to get. I'd always heard that "heat rises," but I was getting *really* warm. I doubted it was just exhaustion, or even just climbing. It was naturally warm. It began to worry me. A dozen fears entered my mind.

What if the heat melts the staircase and we'd all fall to our deaths?

That would pretty much suck. I looked up, still amazed at how much further it went. I thought I could see a hazy outline of the end.

Flitch looked down. He shook slightly.

"Don't look down. We'd die if we fell, and there's only about eight inches of frozen water keeping us up!"

Naturally, I looked down. It was dizzying. The view was amazing, complete symmetry. Very cool. I was sure that almost nothing could compete with it. It was beautiful—simply amazing. It should be called a wonder of the modern wor— Dream Realm.

We climbed for what seemed like several hours. It was hard, tiring work, and not easy.

I fell into a trance. Climbing was hypnotic. The sound of our feet on the steps, and our breaths seemed to synchronize, magnified and silenced at the same time by the enormity of this frozen wonder. Several hundred steps later, we reached the top.

The Dreamers
Chapter 17

What a view! What we saw was even more amazing than the staircase, if that was even possible. We came out on the top of a mountain and along the mountain's ridge, stretching as far as I could see in either direction, was, well, what looked like the Great Wall of China. Complete with battlements! Except that it was made completely out of ice!

What we saw beyond the wall took my breath away. Now in the evening, a crescent sun slowly dipped under the horizon, casting its reflection onto a million different waves. I'm not usually very sentimental, but this was beautiful! Beautiful in a postcard, or screen saver sort of way.

That is, if it weren't for the dam. The dam was a right old ugly piece of work. It was gray cement, dripping and stained with black tar. It stretched along the whole coastline, and was topped with watch towers and barbed wire fences

Oliver Dahl

that protected it from... polar bears? Even from where we were, I could hear the churning sound of motors running.

The dam was nearly as tall as the mountain we were on! The side facing us was supported with large, rounded cement columns. Each the size of a ten story apartment building.

I looked over the edge of the wall to the base of the dam. No water was being let through. I had a feeling that this was Malfix's creation. I had no clue what he had in mind, but was sure that it was nothing good.

"Dam." Flitch said. He said it kind of strangely, so I thought he was pointing it out. I was about ready to reply to him, "No, really?" but then I got the joke. I busted out laughing. I think even Thep smiled a little bit.

"Yup. A big one." I replied, still smiling.

"What do we do?" Flitch asked.

"Infiltrate the dam." Thep said, shaking his head in amusement.

"For that we'll need a dam tour guide." Flitch said. We busted out laughing again, and Flitch had a big smile on his face. Thep just groaned.

"But how, is what I meant." I interjected, stifling laughter.

Thep began nodding. "I have a few ideas."

The Dreamers
Chapter 18

We made base under an especially large tower along the Great Wall of the Ice caves. There was a large window in the tower that allowed us to see the dam. It hurt your eyes to look at something so dark, in all of this ice and snow.

Based on the size and shape of the dam, and Thep's knowledge, we made a guess as to what the inside would look like. Or, at least, a very vague outline.

We sat under a tall tower of the "great wall of ice" while Thep hatched his plan.

"Why is it so hot here?" I interrupted. "It's humid, too."

"I read somewhere that the first Dreamer cast some sort of spell or something that made it warm." Flitch said.

"So! You *can* read?" Thep teased. "Let's focus here, we don't know when *Malfix's* plan could come into play, or even what it is.

Oliver Dahl

We settled on a plan. Thep gave us our assignments, things to bring back with us when we woke.

I was supposed to bring chains, like the ones you put on your tires in the winter.

Thep was supposed to bring C-4. This confused me. First of all, I really didn't know if it would be strong enough to destroy the dam. Thep assured me that it would only take some well-placed structural damage do bring the dam down with all the water it was holding back. I hoped he was right.

Second of all, I had *no idea where* Thep would get it. Oh well, I guess I can't know everything.

Yeah, this would be interesting. As if on cue, I heard a voice in my head calling, "Sam… dinner!" the Dream Realm faded as I returned to earth. The timing was perfect, and I had a job to do.

The Dreamers
Chapter 19

I awoke groggy. I could hear my mom's impatient footsteps coming up to my room.

"Sam!" She called in her "you're in trouble" voice. I quickly wiped up my chocolate-smeared face and ran outside, shutting my door to prevent her from seeing the candy wrappers on the floor.

My mom had been about to open my door.

"Oh…um.…"

"Sam Kullen, I've been trying to call you down for dinner. What've you been doing?"

I couldn't exactly say, "Oh, just planning to destroy a dam!"

"Homework." I replied simply.

"Well then why didn't you hear me call you down for dinner?" Mom asked, obviously PO'd.

"I just had two more problems left; I didn't know they'd take this long." I amazed myself sometimes, at how good my excuses were.

My mom seemed to believe me. She sighed.

Oliver Dahl

"Something is different about you Sam. I don't know what." An idea popped into her head and she looked shocked at it.

"You're not on drugs are you?" She asked nervously.

"Drugs? What! Mom, no! I would never do that!"

"I don't know, Sam. You've been so...not *you* for the past week. Tomorrow I'm going to make an appointment with the doctor. Now get downstairs and *eat your dinner!"*

I hadn't seen my mom like this since the time I used the garden hose to fill up the gas tank in her car—what? I was six! She must *seriously* think something is wrong with me. What if the doctor discovered I was a Dreamer, somehow? Our secrets would be exposed and we'd be tested on. We might become the medical phenomenon of the century! We would be dissected and our brains put in jars. See how my imagination gets away from me sometimes? I began walking to the staircase. A picture frame stood on an end table. I froze. I knew that face.

Funny, cause I'd lived here, my room right next to the end table, and I had never noticed the picture.

"Mom? Who's that?" I asked.

"Don't you change the subject!"

The Dreamers

"No, Mom, I'm not, who is it?"

"You were too young to remember when he died. He was your dad's dad."

Climbing down the stairs, I decided I had to tell my mom the truth. She was right behind me, but I decided to do it over the dinner table. I quickly ran over to the dining room and took a seat. My mom quickly sat back down in front of me.

Her lips were pursed and she was frowning. I knew she was in a bad mood.

"What took you so long?" Cynthia asked impatiently. I pretended I hadn't heard her. I scooped myself some casserole and took a bite.

"Mom…" I began. "The reason I've been acting different is…" I tried to finish by saying, "I'm a Dreamer." But it didn't seem possible to say it. I wanted to tell the truth, but I heard Thep's voice in my head, yelling at me, "No, Sam! You cannot tell her the truth. Tell her… tell her that you are just very tired recently."

"I've been acting differently because I've just been really tired and hungry." I had the sudden urge to yawn and I did.

"I mean, I have to wake up so early for school, and then I'm up late doing homework, I don't have a lot of time for sleep. I'm just… groggy." I finished lamely. I crossed my fingers

Oliver Dahl

under the table, hoping that it would work. My mother looked relieved.

"Okay, Sam. Thanks for telling me the truth. I think we could all use a bit more sleep. After Dad gets home, let's all head to bed early."

I nearly sighed in relief, but that would have ruined me.

"That sounds good." I replied, trying to stop a smile from ripening on my face.

The rest of the meal was spent in silence. The rest of the evening seemed to fly by. Everyone was ready for bed by 8:00.

I listened closely and groaned when I heard my dad turn on the TV. He ran through the channels and fortunately, nothing must have been on, so he eventually went to bed. I sighed with relief. My plan was still possible. I wouldn't have to wait for another hour or so.

I quickly tiptoed down the stairs, avoiding the third step (because it was kind of squeaky) and went out to the garage. Not knowing where to look, I rummaged through the garage, quietly. After digging through some of my dad's camping equipment, I found the tire chains next to the winter clothes corner of our small, two-car garage.

Relieved, I snuck back to my room and placed them on my bed. Not sure what exactly to do, I lied down on my bed. I fell asleep next to

The Dreamers
some old chains. They smelled slightly of gasoline, and it made my nose wrinkle in disgust.

Comfy.

Chapter 20

So… time to get into the dam. Right.

When I awoke—I mean—you get the idea. I was in our base. I didn't know how it knew where to put me, whatever "it" was. It was handy.

It was a dark and stormy night....

Stereotypical? Hey, it was.

My tire chains were with me. I was evidently the first one to arrive. I had fallen asleep at about 9:30, so I was probably half an hour early.

Soon, though, Thep appeared with his C-4 explosives and two shovels. Moments later, Flitch appeared with a hoe and a rake, along with his wire cutters. I asked Thep how he could talk to me in my mind. He simply replied, "Dreamer telepathy."

Thep then took charge.

"Good to see you all managed to bring your things. It's just after nightfall, so we don't have a minute to spare. You both know the plan. We don't

The Dreamers

need to review. Let's go. We need to be both fast and efficient—let's do this!"

At that, I handed my first chain over to Flitch. We had decided that he was the best thrower, (playing baseball and all). He nodded thanks and positioned himself at the edge of the wall.

Our plan was to cause a short on the upper half of the dam. When we threw the chain, we hoped to have it dangle from the electric wires to the metal rim, and cause the power to go out on top. This should, in theory, cause the single guard to leave his post and go to a guard tower to call in help.

While it was dark, we would teleport onto the dam, hoping that the guy wouldn't see us as we sneaked in, as he would be busy phoning in electricians to fix the short.

There was a lot of hoping, and relying on luck. Of course, the chains might not even short the circuit, or, even worse, we might not be able to escape from the dam and we'd all die in the explosion, but, no sense dwelling on that. That's where the luck came in.

Thep swung the chain around, almost like a lasso, and threw it across the ravine.

It hit the fence, three wires at the same time, and caused sparks to fly. As it fell, it drooped over the bottom rung and brushed the metal rim of the dam.

For some reason, this reminded me of that game "ladder ball" or something, where you throw the rope (with two balls on the end) and try to get it on to a PVC pipe goal, each line worth a certain point value. In a way, I guess, it *was* like that, but much more was at stake.

As the two metals met, blue sparks flew, creating shadows in the sudden darkness. It worked? I was incredulous! I had doubted that it would work, but, apparently, it just had!

The guard jumped. He was immediately running toward a guard tower.

Ignoring the last two chains I had brought, (I couldn't find the fourth) I grabbed Thep's hand with Flitch, and we were off over the abyss, and on to the dam.

The Dreamers
Chapter 21

The second we touched the top of the dam, we were all running. We slowed to a jog, trying to find an entrance in the midst of our self-imposed darkness. I hoped the guard didn't have a flashlight. ...Or a backup generator.

After a minute or two, we reached a small structure that looked like an outhouse, or a port-a-potty. (Though it didn't have a crescent moon carved into it or anything). Thep nodded.

"This is it, but...not quite right. We thought that the entrance would be much closer to the edge of the dam. This is pretty far away from it. I'm beginning to think that this isn't what we thought it was." The words were eerie and I shivered.

So, having found the entrance, of course we opened the door and climbed down the stairs. Automatic lights turned on.

This was quite a bit different than the maze we had been in. For one, this place had freshly

Oliver Dahl

replaced bulbs, lined straight, and not one of them flickered or swung slowly in a breeze. Instead of dark, dirty, and mysterious halls, these were bright, and clean, reminding me of a hospital, or school.

I wished this were a school, and that I was a simple student going to third period, not a Dreamer trying to destroy a dam.

Several hallways branched off this main one. Doors blocked them, but I doubted they were locked.

To my horror, a guard, or worker, or somebody walked out of one of these halls. Fortunately, we were lucky, and he didn't notice us! I wasn't sure that that was even possible! The guard crossed the hall, whistling, pulled open another door, and disappeared.

"We should follow him. He looks like a mechanic, and could be going to the engine room." Flitch voted.

"Sounds good to me. Better than getting lost in this place." I chipped in.

Thep nodded in agreement. We opened the door, and walked down a long hallway, half running as we did so. We hit a fork. *Now* it was reminding me of the maze. I looked either way, and saw the door on our left close.

"This way!" I shouted, regretting it, instantly. "Sorry," I apologized, whispering. I could have just blown our cover, and that was something we did *not* need.

We opened the door quietly, just in time to see the worker take another right. We stayed where we were for a little while. We counted about thirty seconds, and then moved on and found a metal staircase. It was ugly, and it appeared as if someone had attempted to paint it red, but had dramatically failed.

It was a hideous piece of workmanship, to be sure. Upon seeing it, I couldn't help but think of the beautiful staircase on the other side of the ravine. But this thing...it's just plain ugly.

"Malfix is no great builder." Flitch commented.

I smirked. "You can say that again!" Thep nodded.

The stairs went down for a hundred steps or so, turned ninety degrees, and continued a hundred more. On and on until my ears popped and I could hear motors whirring and giant turbines running.

I caught a worried look on Thep's face.

"What's wrong?" Flitch asked urgently. He had obviously seen Thep's expression as well.

"We entered the dam very close to the edge. And now... now there's water around us. I think it is wider on top, and gets thinner, but then has a wider base. This is much, much, different than what I thought."

I felt like an idiot for not discovering this before.

"Wouldn't this be a good place to lay the explosives, then. If it's thinner here?" Flitch asked.

"It's as good of a place as any...." Thep mused.

"Well then," I asked. "What are we waiting for?"

The Dreamers
Chapter 22

From here on out, our plans were ultra-simple. We would lay the C-4, and run like heck to escape. Thep would then zap us back over the ravine, detonate the C-4, and then take us to the Dreamer HQ.

All along both sides of the corridor, cement casings surrounded lights that shone up, out of them. A light was placed every four feet or so in the cement casing. The bulbs cast the light on the walls, and that was how we could see. So, that's where we set the C-4.

"This is *too* easy." I said, but I wasn't complaining. Thep and Flitch nodded in reply.

We sat back for a while and admired our handiwork. Well, it was barely visible. You could only tell it was there if you were looking for it. So I guess *that's* what we were admiring.

Now we had nothing to do but escape. Hopefully it would be as easy as getting in. Our luck ran out about half way up the staircase. Why is it that luck *always* runs out?

Bright lights began to flash, and a loud alarm blared overhead.

In the open space behind and below us, guards with guns clamored around like wasps.

Rattatat, rattatat! Machine gun bullets ricocheted around me. Many bullets hit the staircase and pinged, and echoed. The staircase itself shook slightly.

"Run!" Thep shouted, but we already were. We ran for our lives, zigzagging to avoid being hit. The red on the staircase wouldn't be symbolic for long, I feared.

I felt like Indiana Jones at the beginning of Raiders of the Lost Ark, when he was dodging the poison darts. Fortunately, the guys shooting at us were lousy shots.

Either way, I was unscathed. That is, until I tripped on a stair, fell on my face, and smashed my nose. I began sliding backward, scraping my knees as I did so.

"No!" I shouted, clawing at the stairs, trying desperately to stop myself.

"I'll save you, buddy!" Flitch shouted.

Like in a movie, he jumped in slow motion, bullets just missing him, and he landed on the stair above me. He grabbed me and ran up the stairs.

The Dreamers

Flitch quickly caught up to Thep. We were almost to the top!

Suddenly, a spray of bullets passed us, one grazing Flitch's arm, leaving a three-inch gash.

Flitch shouted in pain, but pushed onward.

The sound of the rapid gunfire along with Flitch's shout of pain made a horrible cacophony of sound. I felt like adding to it, but couldn't.

I tried to block the sounds out, but it was impossible! I think I began to cry, but I don't remember.

I barely recall Thep closing the hall door, and the sudden dents of parts of the door as bullets hit it.

We reached the top of the dam, and Thep pushed us aside.

"Look out!"

Scurrying to get out of the way, I pushed Flitch out of danger as well.

I propped myself against a wall, and watched. That was literally all I could do. I seemed frozen in time. I couldn't move—nor did I really want to.

The door of the "port-a-potty" slammed open, and out came Malfix. His albino hair and cool, evil eyes searched the scene. His cloak seemed to be smoldering—smoking and sending off sparks.

"Thep...." He mused. He then nodded briskly, and the two men walked a good distance away. What followed would be the makings of my first witnessed Dreamer duel.

The Dreamers
Chapter 23

Malfix stood near a guard tower. Thep walked briskly up to him. The two bowed in unison. They quickly snapped back up, and retreated about ten paces each. A half sphere, like a snow globe, appeared around them.

Thep put his right hand outward to the side. Malfix did the same. Both performed an impressive move with their hands, using intricate finger patterns and arm motions. A white staff appeared in Thep's right hand, Malfix's a black one. Each staff had a purple glowing sphere on the end. Thep twisted his, and Malfix jabbed his to either side.

Both men then turned sideways, their right foot pointing forward, and their left foot pointing left, their staffs pointed at the other.

Malfix suddenly stabbed his scepter into the ground, and instantly a ring of fire appeared around him. He gave a dark, evil, sardonic laugh.

How original, I thought sarcastically. *Every*

bad guy does that! At least, in all the movies *I'd* seen.

Thep pointed his staff at the ring of fire; it exploded in size, and got taller until it encased Malfix in a flaming "snow" globe of doom. Though, instead of snow, came ashes.

I could see through the flames, and saw that Malfix poked his staff at the top of the fire globe. It turned to ice and shattered.

I could imagine Malfix saying, "You're no match for me, Dreamer!" But, of course, only stereotypical bad-guys would say that.

Nevertheless, that's *exactly* what Malfix said. If I weren't in a sort of vegetative state, I would have laughed. I thought that that was only in movies and stuff. I stand corrected. Maybe some stereotypes are true, after all. (About villains, that is).

Thep made an elephant appear out of nowhere, and Malfix summoned a jet-black jaguar. The jaguar slowly paced around Thep's elephant.

Thep turned the beast into a rabbit, then Malfix turned Thep's elephant into a carrot, and the rabbit ate it.

This continued for a long while, each magician turning the other magician's creation into something else. Yet there I sat, entranced, hypnotized. Neither magician could seem to take

The Dreamers

advantage of the other. They were apparently well matched. I had to do something....

The thought flashed in my mind. *The explosives!* The guards might have found them by now, and they could be dismantling them as I sat.

There, under Flitch, was the detonator. I struggled hard, like I was on the billionth push-up. I pushed against my mind like trying to free myself from heavy chains.

I was able to move, and realized that I was about to become part of the battle.

I reached under Flitch, my heart pounding. I found it. I pulled it out. All I had to do was push the button, but I didn't want to do it in silence. I had to show off, to show that I was a worthy opponent.

"Hey bozo!" I shouted. Okay, not the best insult, let alone the best idea, I know.

Thep and Malfix turned, each with a different expression on his face.

Thep smiled at what he was seeing, and Malfix screamed.

"No! No!" His cry was high and sharp, like a whistle. It was a tortured shriek that reminded me of nails on a chalkboard, and bending metal, and all things that raised the hairs on your body.

Thep jumped toward us, landed on both of us, and we reappeared on the ice caves.

Oliver Dahl

Still hearing Malfix's anguished cries, I raised my fist like I was about to yell a battle cry, and quickly brought my fist down and pushed the button. Thus finished the greatest mistake of my life.

The Dreamers
Chapter 24

I waited for several seconds. Nothing happened. I was pretty sure that I was going to be the next one screaming "No!" but then the explosion came.

Orange and black billowed out of the dam, blowing chunks of cement everywhere into the abyss. At first, nothing further happened, but soon thereafter, cracks became visible.

The cracks spider-webbed randomly through the dam. A last, deep, resounding "thud" reverberated from the dam and it crumbled into the ravine.

Water once again surged freely below the Ice Caves. But... something was wrong with the water. Steam billowed up from it!

Malfix's cold laugh proved me right. His screams were fake—acts to help persuade me to help him.

"Well done, little hero! You have just destroyed the Ice Caves, giving *me* power over it!" Malfix pointed somewhere to my left. I turned and looked at it.

In the distance, I saw a flicker of blue, our flag, being replaced with black. We had lost this one. And it was all my fault. I pushed the button, and condemned the Ice Caves to Malfix. The beautiful staircase, the Ice Caves themselves, the Great Wall of the Ice Caves, it was all going to be destroyed. The beauty of it all simply turned into water.

Malfix's maniacal laughter swept away my thoughts, just as the dam-heated water would the Ice Caves.

I felt so guilty, like I had destroyed a national monument, or a state park. The guilt inside of me was immense, and I sat down and sobbed because of it.

Malfix had disappeared to who-knows/cares where, and Thep ran to Flitch and I. He grabbed both of our hands, and transported us to the Dreamers Headquarters. As we vanished, I saw the Ice Caves sliding into the now warm Ceruvian Sea, never to be seen again.

~D~

The Dreamers

My eyes opened and saw nothing but the familiar light bulb of my own room. I sighed in relief. It was Sunday morning. I never wanted to sleep again. I felt so bad. The time was just after four in the morning.

The guilt inside of me seemed ready to rip its ugly little head out of my stomach and devour me. I felt *so* bad.

I tried to reason with myself, *Sam, you couldn't have known that Malfix intended to destroy the dam,* but then I realized there had been clues that told us that Malfix was heating the water—the steam, the moisture in the air, the heat.

So I just lied on my bed, feeling like crap. I would drink Red Bull, and down 5-Hour Energies so that I never again had to sleep. Maybe I could get used to *not* sleeping, so I could consume something other than energy drinks.

I moped around my room, feeling worthless, until I realized that I *had* to go back. Maybe I could redeem myself by saving the Floating Peaks! I sat up straight, suddenly more awake, and reached for my treat bucket. All guilt gone, replaced with a glimmer of hope.

Chapter 25

Once again, I "awoke" just where I needed to be. I was right in the middle of mission control.

I could immediately tell that the place was different. There was a whole aura to the place. Looking around, I could easily identify it. It was the aura of confusion, bafflement, sadness, and even a little anger.

Dreamers everywhere—more than I had seen in one place ever before—sat in chairs and tables like you might see at a restaurant, with faces of sadness.

Thep nodded to me solemnly from the other side of the room, I quietly walked there, feeling like I ought to be silent, like the feeling you get when you're in a library. Fellow Dreamers nodded grimly as well. I stood against the wall with Thep and Flitch.

"What's going on?" I asked Thep.

Flitch answered for him. "Everyone's

The Dreamers

confused, and sad at the loss of the ice caves. We dunno what to do next."

A tiny bit of guilt came back, but I pushed it away.

"So... everyone's just... mourning?" I asked.

"Basically... but it's a bit deeper than that. We're also trying to figure out what the heck to do next. Whether to attack Malfix, or wait for him to do it. We don't know."

I nodded understanding. I sighed, then cleared my throat to speak. Immediately, everyone's eyes were on me. It was very unsettling.

"Um..." I began. A very... humble beginning.

"What we must do next is very simple. We wait for Malfix to attack."

Immediately, some heads were nodding, others shaking their heads, and voicing *their* opinion.

"But head-quarters could be seriously damaged!"

"We would have the element of surprise if we attacked!"

I forced my way back into the conversation. "Listen up—if Malfix *really* wants control of the Dream Realm, and earth—and we all know he *does!* —then we should know he's going to attack, and that he's going to attack soon. Hopefully not *too* soon, though. The more time we have to prepare, the better. However, Malfix is smarter than that. He will probably try to attack while we're still mourning over a lost territory. We need to forget about that for now, because this battle decides it all!"

By now, everyone was silent, and listening. Unnervingly, the Dreamer Leaders' eyes were on me stronger than ever. I couldn't meet them, yet I couldn't *not* look at them.

"I think that by all means, we should wait—and it shouldn't be long—for Malfix to attack. We have many advantages at our fingertips... height, all that stuff. We can drop bombs, and spread ourselves out, and shoot down there—it'd be easy! Malfix would have to shoot up, which is harder...."

At this point, I was basically bumbling along, making stuff up, and not sounding as firm as I had before. Part of it was the Dreamer Leader's eyes on mine. I was flailing as he stared right through me. I looked back at the Dreamers.

"Look—I feel bad for what I did, but we need to pull ourselves together, and work! We need to be Dreamers! We *need* to be *Dreamers!* We need... to *dream on!"*

That's something for the quote books, there, I thought.

After that it was pretty quiet. People started murmuring again, and I hoped that I had made a

The Dreamers

difference in their opinion. Maybe they were murmuring about what an awesome public speaker I was. (I told you so Mr. Baxter!)

I turned to the Dreamer Leader again. He beckoned for me to come to him. With each step I took, I realized why he looked so familiar.

He cleared his throat. "Sam, I'm so sorry Malfix used you like that. You must feel terrible, and right now, I am telling you that you shouldn't. You were used and it was an accident."

"Why are you telling me this?" I asked, though I knew perfectly well the answer. There was one thing I couldn't stop thinking of.

"Because, Sam... I'm your Grandfather."

The picture on the end table.

Oliver Dahl

Chapter 26

I was stunned, even though I knew with all of my heart that it was true. The picture on the end table, *my grandfather,* was the Dreamer Leader. I didn't how this could be, as my grandfather had supposedly died when I was just a baby.

I hoped the assembly of Dreamers saw my look of surprise. I went on in my admittedly good theatrics.

"Grandpa?" I asked, obvious stun in my voice.

"Yes, Sam." He said sadly. "Sam—I'm so, *so*, sorry. I would *never* do it again if I were given the chance—"

"How, Grandpa?" *Grandpa* felt strange in my mouth. I had never had a grandpa. My mom's dad was the only grandpa I had. Using that word on this virtual stranger was... strange.

"How? You were dead, we thought you were *dead!"*

The Dreamers

My grandfather was silent for a while. Even some of the Dreamers in the mob stopped muttering and looked away, embarrassed.

"Sam... sometimes, as Dreamers, we had to sacrifice our lives in order to help the greater cause. Malfix *must* be stopped. Our lives are at risk in the first place. Sam, we staged my death all those years ago, so that I could devote all the time I had to fight against Malfix. If I had to do it over again, I don't know if I could. Having to miss out on you and your sister's life is almost more than I can live to bear. You are my only grandchildren! I miss your dad so much. I know what I did tore him apart mentally and emotionally. Everyone needs loved ones... life wouldn't be worth living without them—dreams wouldn't exist if not for them, and we had to protect that by doing what we did."

"Wait..." I said. "We? Who else did this?"

Several of the elder Dreamers stepped forward. My heart did a somersault as I saw Thep step forward, an ashen look on his face.

I felt bad again, I felt terribly sad—and yet immensely proud of these men and women. They willingly gave up ever seeing their family and friends again, just to save them in the first place. It was heart-warming.

A single, silent tear fell down my face. I felt like saluting these people, and the honor they exhibited. These people were not afraid—they were strong. They were true Dreamers. These people would fight Malfix to the end of their lives—I knew it. They *did*—and *do*—dream on!

They sacrificed being with their families, to *save* their families. That is a sacrifice made only by the brave. I thought about that. Was I brave enough to never see my family again, but fight so that they could survive? Was I worthy to be one of them?

As before, I began questioning myself, a hundred questions a second. I didn't feel as if I could answer any of them truly.

"I- I don't feel like I belong around you guys. I wouldn't... be able to make a sacrifice like that in a lifetime. I shouldn't be a Dreamer."

"Sam," My grandfather said crisply. "You are just as much a Dreamer as any of us. You stopped Malfix from gaining control over Futurecon, for one. You humiliated him! Malfix televised the whole thing. We saw everything! You were brave, cunning, smart, and more Dreamer than even some of us.

"Sam. You know this. And don't you doubt it for a..." (he swore) "moment!"

I shook my head, "No. I might have been brave, but I *destroyed* the Ice Caves. I didn't just let Malfix have it, I utterly destroyed it! I have no

The Dreamers

idea what I'm doing. This isn't exactly something I can pick up from middle school!"

I was shouting now. I realized my grandfather was crying.

They weren't little sobs, but great, heaving weeps of sorrow that seemed to pull down the fibers of his very being and make his whole body droop like a rag doll. He shook like a volcano, and was just about as loud. His face turned red, and with his teary eyes, he looked at me. His eyes were bright blue, like mine.

"I'm sorry. Sam... I *love* you. You are a great Dreamer." He said. He was still looking straight at my eyes. I knew he was right, and immediately I felt the same way about him. I didn't want him to go. But he did. His head went limp and rested on the back of his throne.

A vertical, burning line appeared above him, it seemed to have been drawn. A curve was slowly added to the right side until it formed a D. Flames must have been symbolic, or something.

It drifted from above my grandpa to above me, where it hovered for a few seconds. My grandfather's body disintegrated into sand and blew away in the wind.

"Grandpa!" I called. That word, that I had only used in front of him twice, echoed in my mind, torturing me, never ceasing in my mind. I kept hearing it over and over... it was haunting and torturing.

I fell to my knees, feeling weak like when I had destroyed the Ice Caves. I had destroyed them, and now I had destroyed my grandfather. Guilt, misery, and sadness—a painful mixture of emotions poured over me.

Suddenly aware of hands on my shoulders, I shrugged them off, staring at the throne that my grandfather had previously occupied.

The Dreamers
Chapter 27

After a few minutes, I became aware of statements that circulated around Headquarters.

"It's a sign," and "He's the next leader." The words passed from mouth to mouth like a game of hot potato.

After, no kidding, five minutes of this, I stood up abruptly, and turned to face them.

I sighed. "None of you even knew me a few days ago, and now I am supposed to be your leader?"

Thep stepped forward. "I will help you in any way I can." He offered. I knew he definitely could—and would.

"I'll do it."

Reflecting back on it, I don't really remember what drove me to make this decision. But later on, I knew I'd made the right one.

~D~

Oliver Dahl

I stood silently, my hands keeping me up, looking out the window. It had begun to rain. It seemed fitting, like the weather was honoring my grandfather's death. Lightning struck, and thunder rumbled. The land far below shook, but the floating islands stayed still.

The rain pattered in through the open window, onto my cold face. I completely ignored it, just as I ignored the feelings inside of me, which were a jumbled length of string.

I welcomed the rain. It replaced my own tears that wouldn't come. The rain refreshed me—revived me... and reminded me. My grandfather's death repeated itself in my mind like a broken record. Over and over again. I couldn't stop it. I tried to force it out, but just couldn't.

I pretended the rain was a shower. It helped clean me emotionally, and physically. I sighed, wondering how I had become destined for *this*.

Thep walked up next to me, put his hand on my shoulder, and shared the rain. Shared the tears. I knew I wouldn't be alone in this position of leadership. I would have help.

"Thep?" I asked.

"Yes, boy?" He replied.

"Why was the 'D' that appeared over him, and the 'D' over my house made of fire?" Luckily, I didn't have to say my grandfather. Thep knew

The Dreamers

perfectly well whom I meant. It was consoling, really.

Thep sighed sadly. I guess you don't really "sigh" any other way, but maybe this sigh was just extra sad.

"When people dream, their dreams usually represent something that they are afraid of, have thought about, or have experienced. And if not their dreams entirely, items or objects from their dreams do. Therefore, the Dream Realm is full of symbolism and representations.

"The flame surrounding the 'D' you saw floating above your house, and just now hovering over your grandfather, represents, or symbolizes, the phoenix. The phoenix is the symbol of the leader of the Dreamers. When a phoenix dies, he is reborn from his ashes. When a leader passes on, a new one is symbolically raised from his ashes. Sam—that's you.

"Come here a moment, in fact." Thep sighed, gesturing for me to follow him. Against my own will, my legs followed him to the throne.

Thep pointed at the throne in general. "What do you see?" He asked.

The throne had small birds, flames, and ashes, all arranged in a perfect cycle carved in the throne.

"I want you to sit in the throne. Just once,

and then if you wish, never again. Please, for me. I need to see it. For me."

I was shaking my head vigorously before Thep even finished.

"Sam. Please." I could see he was nearly breaking into tears.

I sighed in defeat. I slowly placed myself upon the throne. I could feel its coolness through my thin clothes. I put my hands on the armrests, and felt the smoothed surface that had been worn down by dozens of Dreamer leaders before me.

It didn't feel right. I had given nothing more than a restful night's sleep, and I was sitting in a beautiful, golden, throne. Other leaders, like my grandfather, gave up not just a night's rest, but friends and family, ultimately, their lives to be here.

I began shaking my head again at this little thing that shouldn't have mattered. I jumped off the throne and kicked it hard. "I hate it!" I shouted, losing control of my emotions. I drew the eyes of everyone in the room. I bit my lip to keep from screaming again. Everything was so chaotic. So much was going on, my brain couldn't keep up. I almost screamed again.

I wished the flames carved on the stupid throne would erupt, and that the stupid thing would just melt. And then... it actually happened.

The Dreamers

As I thought it, it did just that. I jumped in surprise, shocked. The tiny flames that were carved into the throne, just... came alive, the gold started to melt away. And the flames grew in size, and quickly consumed the whole throne. I wasn't the only one in shock. Everyone in mission control sat, dumbfounded, staring at the flames' curling tendrils. Nobody moved to stop it. If anybody did, I would have assumed that they would fail.

Before long, the chair twisted down into a bubbling mass of gold. The flames abruptly went out. Everyone gasped.

A single word broke the silence.

"Dibs!" It was Flitch, pointing to the puddle of gold on the floor.

"What are we going to do now?" someone asked.

"I'll tell you." I said, disgusted. "We will double our efforts and go after Malfix like never before. He's the reason we fight! He's the reason we can't just enjoy our dreams. He's killed our people. He's trying to take over earth—our families, our friends, everyone on the freaking planet! I say... I say we become his worst nightmare!"

Feeling like finishing with a stereotypical phrase, (since Malfix almost *always* does) I added one last thing.

"So who's with me?"

A long happy cheer erupted from the Dreamers. They were on my side, and we had a battle to win.

The Dreamers
Chapter 28

What followed was a little chaotic. After holding a meeting with all the Dreamers present, we hatched a plan. We learned from our scouts that Malfix was gathering his army and heading our way. It was decided that we should build bridges connecting the floating islands.

Now, I'm not talking cement and steel, we didn't have that kind of time. With the help of the engineers on our side, we started suspension bridges made of rope and planks between several of the islands. The bridges would serve multiple purposes.

First and foremost, since we were able to shoot down Malfix's spies, he didn't know which island the headquarters was on. Having bridges going between several of the islands and with Dreamers battling from all of them, Malfix wouldn't know where to focus his attack. This might buy us more time.

Oliver Dahl

We concluded that the bridges would also give us a tactical advantage over Malfix's army. Having the higher ground and being able to concentrate or spread out our troops as needed made sense. The only problem in the plan was that moving from island to island across the bridges made us more vulnerable as there weren't any places to hide or take cover.

This was war, and this was reality. *My* reality.

Sure I'd ended up as leader, but I didn't really want to have *this* reality. I wanted to be in everyone's normal, every-day reality. I *wanted* school, I *wanted* homework, I *wanted* hundreds of Mrs. Trell's math problems, I wanted all the things that "normal" kids hate. I *wanted* to have big projects and eight pages of math. I *wanted* to be unpopular. I wanted *anything* but this.

I wanted an *escape*. I wanted to be *home.*

I sighed out loud. What wonderful, wonderful words those two are. Escape. Don't you love how it just rolls out of your mouth? It feels natural, and wonderful, nearly as wonderful as the meaning.

Home. The word feels natural in your mouth. However, it brings homesickness and a greater yearning to be there.

I loved those words and would do anything

The Dreamers

to achieve them. I *knew* that I was supposed to do this. I was supposed to beat Malfix, and if that was my destiny—I would *not* back down.

Anyway, while everyone was working on the bridges, I had time to think a little. Three (or was it two? Or five?) days ago, I was just an ordinary kid going to school every day. I teased my sister, hated homework, and couldn't wait until summer break. Now what am I? A freaking leader of some group of people whose main goal in life is to defeat an evil king who wants to be a supreme dictator of an alien world.

Part of me really just wanted to go back home. I'd only been away from home a short time, but I was, yeah, I'll admit it, I was homesick. Would I ever be able to go home to stay? Or would I be like my grandpa and end up living here? I had a lot of questions for Thep.

I was brought out of my daze by the sound of shouting. I came out of my room and saw Dreamers running off in several different directions. Most of them were carrying weapons, supplies—or both. I ran to the closest bridge and looked around. I noticed there were a lot more Dreamers than before—more must have come to fight.

Recognizing many of the faces from book jackets, movie posters, and Popular Mechanics stories. I longed to get autographs, but now was not the time.

I saw lots of people that I didn't recognize, though, and they didn't recognize me. But as word passed on that I was their new leader, I got a lot of encouraging and even curious looks.

I looked towards what everyone else was looking at—the setting sun. Below it, the ground seemed to move.

Malfix's army was here.

The Dreamers
Chapter 29

After we Dreamers had spread ourselves across the floating islands and received weapons, we could do nothing but watch as the sun began to set and the outline of Malfix's army grew. I ordered a few people to give out extra weapons, as it would be needed, and to have extra ammunition handy for when it would become required. Which, I hoped, wouldn't be soon.

The sun's light was gone, and the moon was a quarter way up in the sky. I didn't want to fight during the night; I wanted to be able to see easily. That's what I worried about. I wasn't really tired, as I'd been sleeping on and off the past day or two.

Oh, right. You're probably wondering, "How can you sleep in a dream?" Good point. I don't really know. I remember once I had a dream that I was sleeping. Maybe if you can dream about sleeping, you can sleep in a dream. I asked Thep, and he just said, "It's complicated." He had been saying that a lot, lately. I couldn't really blame him, though, because he was so busy. After that, I didn't waste his time.

Minutes dragged by, and the enemy drew closer and closer. The closer the enemy got, the higher my heart rose into my throat. I was scared. Utterly terrified. There was no way to know what was going to happen.

All too soon, the entire enemy army was right under us. And though they looked small, being several hundred feet below, I felt like we were sitting ducks.

I was enthralled, I couldn't tear my eyes away. I noticed that the enemy lines rippled with people or soldiers disappearing and appearing. When one would go, another would take his place.

Somehow, I knew that this was because the people below us were dreaming. Somewhere else, their body lay asleep, while their mind inhabited a copy of their body—their animated forms. Unlike Dreamers, they couldn't really control their dreams, feel pain, or truly interact with their surroundings. They were just...there.

"Ready!" Thep's voice rang out. The other Dreamers' responded with a loud but simple grunt, "Hut!"

We were the Dreamers, and we were prepared.

The Dreamers
Chapter 30

The sound of Malfix's voice seemed to rip the air in half. I could see him from where I was standing only because the robe he was wearing was on fire. Dark orange flames licked the air around him.

"Dreamers!" He bellowed. "Surrender now and I *will* be merciful...."

As if in one body, the Dreamers cried in unison, *"Never!"*

"So be it." He retorted. He turned back towards his army and shouted, "Destroy them!" He turned back towards us and shot streams of bright yellow flame on the bridges and islands.

All at once, chaos erupted. Battle cries deafened me. The cries were soon obliterated by the sound of gunfire and bombs falling and exploding.

Everything slowed down. Yellow flames billowed around areas of the bridge and quickly faded. Nothing had burnt, but everything smelled strange.

Another, larger yellow roar of flame, and I ducked (okay, I fell...) out of harms way. I flattened myself on the now swinging bridge, sick to my stomach and cooking.

With a cry of alarm, I jumped up, and surveyed darkened spots on my shirt that matched the pattern of the bridge's planks.

I ran toward a pile of light-blue grenades on the nearest floating island. They were stacked in neat little boxes. I picked one up.

I'd seen movies and heard jokes and talk about grenades. Pull the pin, throw it. Right? I hoped so.

Shaking my head in bewilderment, I found a small ring on a clip thing and pulled on it. It didn't come out. I wasn't pulling hard enough. I was afraid it would explode too soon.

Cursing my fear, I pulled harder on it. This time it slid out. I heard a sound and some instinct told me to throw it.

I threw just too late. The thing exploded just under the bridge. I winced and looked around; hoping nobody had seen my epic fail. I probably could have hurt someone pretty bad if I'd thrown it a *second* later. That someone would have probably been me, I realized with a shock

The Dreamers

I quickly came to the realization that I was no grenadier. I looked to my left, toward base. I was amazed and terrified at what I saw. From all around the Floating Peaks, smoke and gunfire could be seen falling or shooting off the bridges. The cascade of projectiles was so thick it nearly blocked the view behind it.

It was terrifying. I didn't want to be here. I urged myself to wake up. No such luck. I began crying, wanting so much to wake up! I couldn't.

Above the din of battle, I heard Thep cry out in pain. Don't ask me how I heard him, or how I knew it was him, I just did. I ran in the direction of the sound, passing by Dreamers who were still fighting for, and literally *dying* for our cause—wanting to help them, but needing to find Thep. I crossed a bridge and to my horror, saw Thep and Malfix engaged in a duel.

"Thep!" I cried, wanting him to know I was there. He was bruised and bloodied, and from what I could see, looked like he wasn't going to last much longer.

I couldn't get to him, as there was a force field around the area. I watched helplessly, pounding my fists against the invisible wall.

Thep looked in my direction, acknowledging my presence, but not exactly seeing me standing there.

Oliver Dahl

Malfix was circling around him like a predator moving in for the kill. He conjured dozens of ninja stars from mid-air and flung them at Thep. With a flick of a nearly broken wrist and a few words, a brick and mortar wall appeared, blocking the shruikans from their intended target.

Malfix chuckled as if he were toying around.

"You are obviously no match for me. Look at yourself! You're at death's door! 'Knock-knock, please *do* come in!'" With a flourish, Malfix slammed Thep into a large steel door that appeared.

"Oh, did I forget to open it?" Thep collapsed to the ground, barely breathing, his body broken. Malfix noticed me at last. He looked back in Thep's direction and made the steel door, (that looked like it belonged on a vault in a bank) fall over and crush Thep. Malfix chuckled and sent lava over the door—and Thep. It cooled quickly, forever encasing Thep.

The Dreamers
Chapter 31

Malfix laughed wickedly.

"Dreamer," He spat, refocusing his attention on me.

"You're the one who unwittingly helped me destroy the Ice Caves, aren't you?"

I stared at him angrily.

"I never had the chance to thank you. You ran off before I could express my appreciation." His face melted into a widened grin.

Anger and rage were boiling up inside of me. I was oblivious to my surroundings. By now, all of the bridges were on fire and most (if not all) the Dreamers were dead or dying.

"I *told* you I'd be merciful if *only* you'd surrender." He said mockingly. Remorselessly he added, "If only you had listened to me, then all of this could have been avoided."

"*Liar!*" I yelled, finally finding my voice.

"Now, now, that's not how you treat the

emperor of the Dream Realm," Malfix cooed, shaking his pointer finger back and forth—like scolding a child!

He then snarled and hugged himself. He then moved his arms out quickly, and all the bridges and floating peaks burst into orange flame, if they had not been already.

He saw me flinch. He laughed. With a twist of his hand, he forced me to turn toward the burning scene. He didn't allow me to blink or turn my head. He had control and made my eyes turn left and right, forcing me to take it in. I hated it. It was something out of a horror movie, the climax of a chiller. It was horrible, ugly, violent, and should only have been made in the first place by Hollywood props and dummies. I knew they weren't though, and that's why it was so bad.

"You destroyed the Ice Caves. And now, you have given me the power to destroy the Floating Peaks. Once I kill you, there will be no Dreamers left. I can easily reclaim Futurecon, and then the Dream Realm will officially be mine!" The dork sounded like the stereotypical bad guy he was.

Malfix's horrible speech added to the terror of the scene that lay before me. Now, instead of weapons and bombs falling off the bridges, I saw that Dreamers were. They were jumping off, unable to withstand the heat.

The Dreamers

I began to cry again. "You are a wicked, evil man!" I screamed. I tried to spit in his face, but it only dripped off my chin. I hardly noticed—or cared, really.

"Why, thank you," Malfix said, bowing his head in mock gratitude. "I take it as a compliment, though, I want to be known as the rightful ruler of the Dream Realm. Not some vicious killing machine..." Malfix said.

"You can't deny that that's what you *are!*" I seethed, looking over at the vault door lying flat on the ground, under all the lava.

"You've got a point," Malfix gave in, taking a stance similar to the one he had prior to killing Thep.

"Let's get this over with. Once *you're* out of the way, there'll be *no one* left to stop me."

The sun was just beginning to rise. The battle had lasted all night. Bigger and bigger, groups of Malfix's army were disappearing without replacements filling in the ranks. Malfix didn't look worried. If there were any Dreamers left, I was the only one in good enough condition to fight. He didn't need his army anymore.

This was going to be just between the two of us.

Chapter 32

A part of me didn't believe that I could be the last, but a single glance at all the carnage around me clearly said, "You're the last, so don't try to run and hide from me."

This was it. The final showdown. What happened here decided it. I was the last living Dreamer. Every Dreamer had come to fight, and they had all died, fighting for our cause—except for me. It pains me to write this. Though I didn't know many of them, I knew that somewhere, they had a family and a history. Some of them could have unfinished novels, or inventions. One of them could have become an award-winning architect had they not died.

I was the last one.

Malfix turned his gaze on me. I was chilled at the anger his glare emanated. I was the only and last thing standing in his way. Once he killed me, there was nothing further to stop him. The Dream

The Dreamers

Realm and the world would be his. I couldn't imagine what would happen if Malfix ruled the world. It would be terrible.

A simple duel was all that stopped this.

The thing with a Dreamer duel is this: it's completely random and you are only as powerful as your imagination. From what I saw of the duel between Thep and Malfix, Malfix had a sick imagination. I say random because you basically imagine things flying at or happening to your opponent, and he just tries to block or prevent those things by imagining some kind of defense.

So... I had a pretty good idea what to do, just not how to do it. I thought about the flames from the throne coming to life and reducing the seat to a puddle of gold, and how I wished that it would resume its original form.

Malfix spoke. "Tell you what, since this is your first time, I'll let you go first." He obviously thought I didn't know what I was doing. He was partially right, but I hated his sarcastic offer. I decided to be a little creative and give him a slap in the face—literally. No sooner had I thought it, than a hand appeared out of nowhere and slapped him right across the face, then disappeared. Malfix was shocked, almost as much as I was.

While Thep and Malfix had to do intricate hand movements or gestures, all I had to do was think about it for it to happen. It was pretty awesome, I must admit.

This might not be as hard as I had thought. Anything that Malfix threw at me, (from poison darts to shards of broken glass) I simply turned into those Styrofoam packaging peanuts. My opponent didn't look too happy. As he tried harder and harder to get to me, the objects became more and more nonsensical. Office chairs, toothpicks, a pack of squirrels, printer cartridges, and hardback novels were just some!

Next, I imagined a barrier around me that would keep all of Malfix's projectiles from reaching me. After a demolition ball, tidal wave and curtain rungs hit my barrier and fell harmlessly to the ground, two thoughts came into my head.

First, Malfix was stubborn and was never going to stop trying to kill me, and I better stop playing only defense.

Second, if my barrier would keep things out, would the reverse be true? I imagined an indestructible, but invisible, box around Malfix.

His next attack was stopped. The box caused the... chainsaws?! ...to rebound toward him. He froze them in mid-air and they clattered and shattered at his feet.

"You... you fool!" Malfix raged, though his voice was blurred through the box. He had

The Dreamers

obviously not planned for this. I thought fast. I imagined the box stronger—now he wouldn't be able to use his powers on outside things, like me.

Malfix didn't detect this, and he tried to attack me with a swarm of angry wasps. They appeared *in* his box—and not outside. My plan was working.

I would have thought that somebody would have thought of trapping an opponent in a box before, but apparently, it had not been done, so it wasn't expected.

It was extremely effective. After Malfix had been stung a few dozen times, he caused the wasps to spontaneously combust. He knew he could do nothing further.

Malfix's raged screams were silenced behind the box.

I had an idea. I didn't want to hear, or see it, though.

Making the box so Malfix couldn't see out, and I couldn't see in proved to be fairly easy. I then made the box soundproof. This, too was simple.

I swallowed hard, and closed my eyes. I imagined the box shrinking. Cruel? Yeah, it was, but I couldn't just open the box, pat him on the back and let him go!

I peeked through slitted eyes and saw the box was about the size of a classroom recycling bin. I braced myself and shrunk the box even smaller.

I stopped when it was the size of a shoebox then I imagined that shoebox under a whole bank vault, not just a door, at the bottom of the ocean. He was gone.

The force field faded, and I was exposed to fresh air. I'd never smelled anything so sweet as the smoke-filled morning air.

I had no one to celebrate with. I stood on a floating island, alone. The fires that my enemy had started were dying out now, just wisps of smoke was all that was left.

All across the peaks, bridges fell, clattering to the ground below.

Above me in the sky a letter "D" hung ablaze in orange flames. To me it symbolized more than the Dreamers. It symbolized victory over evil.

I promised myself I would find new Dreamers to replace those who were killed. With that thought, the insignia burned even brighter. For the first time in what felt like much too long, I smiled.

The Dreamers
Chapter 33

I woke up in bed, not in mine, but in a white, sterilized one. I looked to my side and saw that the bed had guardrails—almost like a crib. Just beyond the rails I saw a machine that had a bunch of wires and cords coming out of it. Most of the cords were hooked to me! It was a heart monitor.

I looked down at myself and noticed I was wearing a hospital gown and I had an IV in my arm.

I figured that my parents must have thought I was in a coma, (I must have been asleep for nearly a week) and had admitted me to the hospital.

I sat up and my mouth tasted like I hadn't brushed my teeth in a week, (which I hadn't, and...gross).

Looking around the room, I saw my dad was asleep in a chair and my mom and sister were sharing a cot.

A nurse was walking by the door and saw me sitting (probably with a rather embarrassing look on my face!) on the bed, perfectly conscious. She stepped away from her cart and opened the door, forgetting that people were sleeping.

The sound of the door opening quickly and the lights turned on soon awoke my mother, father, and sister. Their heads all turned to the nurse, then to me.

"Sam!" My mother cried, running to embrace me.

"Mom—I'm fine! I—" I let her.

"We were so worried about you! What happened?!" My father asked.

"I—" I tried. I couldn't really talk too well. Attempting again, I managed, "I don't really know. I don't remember anything." Even if I *did* tell them the truth, they'd never believe me.

"Well, I'm glad you're okay," My mom said, smiling happily. "Let's get you out of here."

I'd never heard better words.

~D~

After signing a few papers and promising the doctors they'd bring me back for a check-up next week, my parents drove me home. I don't think I'd ever been as excited to walk through my front door.

On the way back, I saw a set of twins rush

The Dreamers

into their front door from school, probably to get ready for football practice. I couldn't wait until I could do the same.

We finally arrived home, and my mom dragged me into the kitchen and fixed me a meal. I guess I hadn't eaten in a week, so she assumed I was hungry. She was right.

After nearly emptying the fridge, I yawned and told her I was tired. She looked at me funny because I had just woken up from a seven-day snooze. She didn't push the issue, though. She was just glad I was home and okay.

I got up to my room, but instead of grabbing a blanket and my pillow, I grabbed a comp notebook and a pencil, sat at my desk, and wrote down everything I could remember about what had happened to me in the Dream Realm... my story.

What you're now holding in your hands is the final copy of that manuscript—with a few things I added that I remembered later. So, even though this is sold as a fictional piece, it's actually one hundred percent true. And if you believe me, you just might have what it takes to become a Dreamer.

Oliver Dahl

The Dreamers

Oliver Dahl
Epilogue

In my dreams, I often find myself in mission control, and see the remains of the throne, the abandoned rooms and halls, stained with soot and ash. Sometimes, I'll just sit, looking out the window where I watched the sunset right before the battle with Malfix's army. I think about Thep, about all the other Dreamers that died, but mainly about Thep.

I'll find myself walking the empty streets of Futurecon, remembering some of Flitch's stupid knock-knock jokes. I have even been back to where the beautiful spiral staircase used to stand. Though it is gone, the remnants of the dam are still there.

Have you ever had a dream that was so vivid that it seemed real? Well... my dreams, the dreams of the Dreamers are like that—but they become real.

I wait, and am looking for, the next genera-

The Dreamers

tion of Dreamers to appear. And when they do, we'll rebuild the Dream Realm together.

I made *my* story great. What will you do with *yours?*

Dream on!
Sam Kullen

Oliver Dahl
Acknowledgments

Thanks for reading this book. That means everything to an author. If anything can surpass that thanks, it is the thank you that comes when you tell your friends, your family, your teachers, your students, and that random guy walking into the mall about this book. Even if it doesn't get one more person to read the book, people will know about it, and that is always good for the author.

I must say, however, that you as the reader and sharer of this book are not the only ones who deserve thanks. *Many* people deserve thanks for this book.

Editors, you're first. You've helped convert this book into something a lot better. You've saved me a lot of embarrassment, too. Thanks to my mom and dad. They helped make the story flow, and make sense in more ways than grammatically. Thanks to Parker Parrish who stayed up all night during that one scout camp out to read this, and who gave me awesome structural advice.

The Dreamers

Others have simply peeked over my shoulder when I've edited and pointed things out that I'd never noticed. You guys helped save me from being humiliated.

Thanks to teachers, principals, fellow students, and *everybody* who supported this story.

And, to cover my bases, I thank everyone who had anything to do with this book. Whether that's putting it through the printer, or glancing at it on Amazon.com or wherever else—thanks!

Oh, an author's note, too: there will be a sequel! Nothing official yet, but I've started brain storming and pre-writing up the sequel, and I think that you'll enjoy it. So, if you liked The Dreamers, grab the sequel when it's out, or visit Sam's blog,

www.thedreamersadventures.blogspot.com

Dream on!
Oliver Dahl

Oliver Dahl

The Dreamers

To view the trailer, or learn more about *The Dreamers* series, view sneak peaks, educate yourself on Sam, Oliver Dahl, and everything else in the Dream Realm, visit Sam's blog:

www.thedreamersadventures.blogspot.com

or

use your smart phone app to follow this QR code: